Ikons

Ikons

MEDITATIONS IN WORDS AND MUSIC

John Tavener and Mother Thekla
with Ivan Moody

Fount
An Imprint of HarperCollins*Publishers*

Fount Paperbacks is an Imprint of
HarperCollins*Religious*
Part of HarperCollins*Publishers*
77–85 Fulham Palace Road, London W6 8JB

First published in Great Britain
in 1994 by Fount Paperbacks

1   3   5   7   9   10   8   6   4   2

Text © 1994 John Tavener and Mother Thekla
Commentary © 1994 Ivan Moody

Photographs of ikons courtesy of The Temple Gallery

John Tavener and Mother Thekla assert the moral right to be
identified as the authors of this work

A catalogue record for this book is
available from the British Library

ISBN 0 00 627871 X

Typeset by Harper Phototypesetters Limited
Northampton, England
Printed and bound in Great Britain by
Scotprint Limited, Musselburgh, Edinburgh

Copyright information on the Compact Disc is
printed at the back of the book

Contents

Introduction

We live in an age when man has lost belief not only in God but also in himself. Metaphysics has been completely split from the world of the imagination. So when I was asked to join music and words in this book and compact disc, it seemed like a heaven-sent opportunity to attempt to explain how I am coming to terms with this malaise, and how a unique collaboration with an Orthodox abbess has inspired and helped me along an almost impossible road.

Mother Thekla came into my life in 1981. I remember ringing the monastery one day, after reading her remarkable work on Mary of Egypt, and asking, 'Is Mother Thekla still alive? If so, I would like to speak to her.' I knew that one of the three nuns had died, and I was not sure whether it was Mother Maria, Mother Thekla or Mother Katherine. Mother Katherine answered the phone, and called Mother Thekla in from the garden. She seemed to think that some kind of 'collaboration' might be a possibility but 'behind the scenes', so to speak. Four years passed before we actually met. We communicated by telephone – almost daily, in fact, particularly when my own mother was dying.

Few composers can have been blessed by finding a librettist, a spiritual mother, and a tireless correspondent all in one person! Mother Thekla soon convinced me of the 'nonsense' (in my case) of seeking to take monastic vows and, at the same time, convinced me of the 'nonsense' of composing purely liturgical music 'for a church that was not ready for it'. Our first major collaboration was with her translation from the Russian of *The Akathist of Thanksgiving*: 'Glory to God for everything' – the dying words of the martyr St John Chrysostom, and used by Archpriest Gregory Petrov as he awaited death in a Siberian prison camp. 'The text is quite good,' Mother Thekla said, having seen the original Russian, 'but I can improve on it!'; and so she did, with a long commentary (in green biro!) making all the liturgical links.

This was invaluable to me, and so were all the hints in the text of double movement, Cross Resurrection, belief – unbelief and so on. I was beginning to build up a language of musical symbolism and metaphor that could search out the inner meaning, the theology and the philosophy of the text. Body and mind are not the man, but only his instrument and vehicle. Blake is in accord with these traditional dicta when he equates 'the divine acts of imagination' with Christianity itself and asks, 'Is the Holy Ghost any other than an intellectual fountain?'

It was on this level that we communicated. Mother Thekla was not a musician, but what I needed most was someone with whom I could check 'philosophical certitude', in so far as this is possible within the limitation of the human mind. To 'think for oneself' is always to think of oneself; what is called 'free thought' is therefore the natural expression of a humanistic philosophy. We are at the mercy of our thoughts and corresponding instincts. Free thought is a passion; it is much rather the thoughts than ourselves that are free. Mother Thekla taught me this in a quite simple and non-didactic way. 'I am depressed', I might say to her. 'Why shouldn't you be?' she would reply. This answer linked me to the heart of Orthodox ascetic spirituality.

I think that both of us agreed that it was necessary to move out of 'the Church' back into 'the market-place', to fill the *temeaos* (an ancient Greek word meaning sacred space) with a language of symbolism and order that I had learnt from the immeasurable depths of the Orthodox Church and that I wished to try to communicate to my hypothetical secular audience. Somehow there must be an intelligibility and functional efficiency in the music. The intelligibility of traditional art does not depend on recognition but, like that of script, on legibility. So, symbols are the universal language of art: an international language with merely dialectal variations.

Of course we never thought like this at the time! God forbid! But with hindsight I can see that this was the direction in which we went, and are still trying to move. No wonder *Die Zauberflöte* (The Magic Flute) is the only opera both Mother Thekla and I can stand, because the content of symbols, however naïve and ridiculous, is metaphysical.

Mother Thekla has no real pride in the work she does for me. She is prepared to write, rewrite, cut down and extend *ad libitum*. This is a real gift for a composer, when he is so often bogged down with verbose texts and in despair at what to do with them. Often a text will come back through the post from Whitby after the sixth amendment with 'I *will not* write it again.' Normally she is right – it cannot be pared down any further without losing the sense.

The artist is constantly represented as imitating heavenly forms: therefore the references of symbolic forms must be as precise as mathematics. We are in total harmony about this and Mother Thekla is a kind of spiritual Agatha Christie forming mathematical links, connecting the unlikely with the likely, seeing all kinds of surreal-istic illusions, and then saying 'full steam ahead' to me to work with a musical symbolism that can reach from New Orleans to New Delhi – symbolism drawn from the West, Byzantium and the Sufis; from this tapestry 1 try to make a totally integrated synchronistic whole.

But how many have talked about a perennial philosophy? Can there really be a 'perennial music'? Yes, musically 1 believe that there can be, provided the music is fully integrated. Mother Thekla soberly cautions me with the severe dictum 'that we must suffer the split, and suffer the fall in all its implications'. Here is the *via negativa* side by side with the *via positiva*. Yet God is an objective reality, and it does not matter whether Tom, Dick or Harry believes in Him or not. He is beyond good and evil, and He exists. In fact, He is the only one who can possibly say *Egó íme*: 1 am.

And yet, the further we advance along the road of metaphysics the greater the sense of 'not knowing'. In awe and terror-stricken, we stand with the Mother of God at the Annunciation and say with her 'How can this be?' And then with Plato 'across the frozen chain of centuries', we say 'Let us begin again!'

Let us begin again and again and again, but let us always begin again as if for the first time, picking up all that we have learnt from both the *via negativa* and the *via positiva*. But, as Mother Maria says, 'Let us always crawl on all fours'. The only way forward is the way of repentance. We must never separate our failure from our defeat. Each new piece of music is a 'failure' – 'or not' as Mother Thekla sharply reminds me. We believe and yet we know nothing. We shall see God as He is because it is promised to us, and for no other very good reason than the joy of 'not knowing' and yet believing. Like the suffering in the music of the East, it does not lead to melancholy, nor does its joy bring pounding of the heart. In fact it possesses a kind of 'joy–sorrow' – the sobriety that one finds in all the music of the Orthodox Church. Mother Thekla and 1 are almost incapable of ending on a 'high note'. The text and the music either suggest a question mark, or simply '1 know nothing'.

When 1 write music without text, it is never 'abstract'. There is always intended to be a spiritual meaning. 1 have to understand the ultimate *raison d'être* of every single note, and 1 will telephone Mother Thekla sometimes up to twenty times a day to double-check the *raison d'être* of the musical iconography and just why it is as it is and not otherwise. For instance, *The Protecting Veil* can be listened to by my hypothetical public and though it is not necessary for them to understand the meaning of every note, you can be sure that this has been checked and double-checked during the working process. Once the music leaves my study, however, it leaves my study, and the best that 1 can hope for is that it communicates at a deeper level than just 'like' or 'dislike' – not through any gift of my own but because 1 have used symbols and, if they have been used correctly, then they should transmit a knowledge of cosmic analogies.

I mentioned Mother Thekla's remarkable analysis of St Mary of Egypt – the story of non-judgement, seeming vice and seeming virtue. I wanted a libretto of almost child-like simplicity for my opera – non-didactic. I could not have found a better collaborator than Mother Thekla. As she said, 'the seeming vice of Mary the whore of Alexandria, and the seeming virtue of Zossima, the holy man . . .' the doors were closing on Zossima, but they were an opening to Mary. At least she had the 'one thing needful', however misdirected. And then, after many years, they meet in the desert and utter only one word to each other, 'Bless'. Zossima begins to 'live' again, because he has found 'the one thing needful'.

The musical 'symbolism' for *Mary of Egypt* was very important, but also very difficult, because of all the paradoxes. I remember that we listened to *The Magic Flute* very frequently during this time. Not that *Mary of Egypt* has anything in common with Mozart's magnum opus, but it did seem to be the only Western piece of music that came anywhere near to *Mary of Egypt*. I also read the very early Egyptian Christian fathers, much beloved by me and by Mother Thekla for their ferocity, their lack of banal religious instruction, their piercing simplicity and their infinite compassion, unknown or even imagined by any of us today.

Mother Thekla also gave me a fresh perspective on the Old Testament, always seeing as it were 'through' the New Testament, backwards and forwards. This finds its expression in *The Resurrection*, *The Hidden Treasure*, *Psalm 123* and other pieces, although I had previously written a youthful extravaganza *The Whale* based on the story of Jonah and the whale, which of course prefigures the Passion and Resurrection. And then there is the Passion of Christ, God Himself, relived every year:

I see your Cross, your Cross for my sake.
My spirit is dust before the Cross:
Now is the triumph of love and salvation.
Here praise unto the ages does not cease. Allelujah.

That first balance between Cross and Resurrection – the Gospels are, as Mother Maria says, 'only a beggar's cloak' or, in Mother Thekla's words, 'hints'; the rest is a work. 'To work is to pray, and to pray is to work.' And then there are the 'saints', our guides and future 'hints'.

The Resurrection was a 'work' indeed. Mother Thekla had taken passages from the prophets, the Passion narrative and the Liturgy. Here were my three groups – all characterized by different musical symbols and all coming together in *The Resurrection*. Christ is risen! *Christos Annesti, Christos Bockresi*! Christ is risen and no one is left in the grave. Christ is risen and the demons are fallen! And yet we can only dance inside the Resurrection for a short time – we have not 'grown up' to it. So the Mother of God has the last say – 'Be it unto me according to thy word'.

So, art is essentially symbolic, seeing God as 'light', and only accidentally illustrative or historical. Just as art, even the highest art, is only the means to an end, likewise the Scriptures – a means of 'seeing through a glass darkly'. The traditional artist is not expressing himself, but a thesis. Now the thesis may be obscure, and therefore the manner of expressing it may need to be obscure, but I think that the aspiration of both Mother Thekla and me is to write a kind of metaphysical pantomime full of symbolic and metaphysical meaning, comprehensible to a six-year-old, as well as to a sixty-year-old. This is a huge work, and maybe we shall never achieve it. Even if we were to come near to attaining it, the utility of iconography must one day come to an end and, when we have laid down our pens for the final time, vision will be 'face to face'.

The purpose of this book and CD is to try to give a hint of how it might be possible to reinstate the Sacred into the world of the imagination. Without this happening, I believe that art will continue to slither into a world of abstraction, into being purely self-referential, a sterile and meaningless activity of interest only to the artist and possibly 'Brother Criticus'.

All great civilizations, except the present one, have understood this as a matter of course. We live in abnormal times; as André Malraux has said: 'Either the twenty-first century will not exist at all, or it will be a holy century'.

It is up to each one of us to determine what will happen.

Holiness

The Norman Conquest has been blamed and praised for much of England's subsequent history – political, economic, social, and, of course, ecclesiastical – but I doubt if much thought has been given to its effect on any efforts, nine hundred or so years later, to interpret or translate aspects of Orthodox spirituality, Greek or Slavonic, into English that is comparable with the original.

No doubt partly because of the Conquest, English is an extremely rich language with fine nuances of meaning brought about by the juxtaposition of conqueror and conquered, master and servant. Who else can boast of swine in the field but pork on the table? Sheep to pasture, mutton to eat? House and mansion? Small holding but petty crime? And yet, such nice distinctions, such precise discrimination between the familiar and the official, the day-to-day and the formal, can and do lead to difficulty when faced with something *essentially* simple.

HOLINESS AND SAINTLINESS

Precision of discrimination is an immediate potential drawback to mutual understanding between East and West. In English, 'holy' is, as it were, an informal expression of a spiritual condition but without 'official' sanction. As soon as someone graduates to a technical holiness, he progresses from being a holy man to being a saint; holiness to saintliness – there is a distinct, even formidable barrier between everyday goodness and the leap into official acknowledgement of such goodness. I am not speaking here of the whole procedure of canonization but of the instinctive intellectual reaction to hearing the words 'a holy man' or 'a saint'. One is technically what the other is naturally. Such linguistic discrimination puts an invisible barrier between the possible and the nearly unattainable; it sets a preconceived frontier of goodness, outwardly recognized by a legal process. In effect, it allows for human judgement, the power to weigh, to estimate, the 'value' of a spiritual condition.

THE QUALITY OF HOLINESS

It sometimes seems to me that holiness, the quintessence of holiness, is as elusive as that strange fragrance in the air which heralds spring. We cannot define precisely where the scent lies, nor analyse exactly the colour of buds, nor yet assign to an invisible musical scale the plaintive bleat of a lamb, nor to a paintbox the fleeting blue of the sky: a stirring in the blood, an impulse towards adventure, rough moorland, woodland paths. All not to be defined. With definition, component parts emerge; metal bars, screws, bolts. And is it not so with holiness? Define holiness and what is it but a skeleton formality? Every bone neatly soldered into an ascetic ankle, a spinal cord of meditation, an eye socket awash with humility. No, holiness is not to be defined. It is a living, glorious re-birth; it is an active condition, not a struggle with or against self, but a struggle for self, to bring oneself back, back to that pure and fragrant spring of man's creation.

ASCETICISM

Ascetic efforts are so often totally misunderstood. I do not say wasted; no spurt of love towards God, however ill-judged, misdirected or apparently ineffectual, can be wasted, for He surely accepts it as a love-offering and transfigures it into whatever was intended, not what it may appear in its evident inadequacy. If it seems a little futile to sit on top of a pillar apparently for no purpose, it is not for us to judge the seeming uselessness; usefulness, spiritual or material, is a highly relative commodity. And the apparent uselessness may well be an image of the vanity of human effort: let us sit on top of a pillar and once and for all demonstrate the inadequacy of our lives.

To say, in criticism of such behaviour, that if we all chose to sit on pillars, life would cease and children would starve, is not the point; the fact is that we are not all prepared to do so and that surely leads to one aspect of the Communion of Saints. Some sit on pillars, some work in the fields. I have found that people are only too apt, as a form of reproof, particularly to monks and nuns, to produce this argument repeatedly: 'What would happen if we *all* chose to retreat into monasteries?' The only answer is 'But – we don't!'

THE WORK OF HOLINESS

'Holiness' is a pure, simple word. Yet, although in essence holiness is not to be contained within complications, being, as it is, a resolution of warring qualities within us, yet it may manifest itself in a variety of forms.

First, then, we must recognize that all conscious striving towards purity of life is not the ruthless extirpation of all natural feelings, emotions, endeavours, appetites; if it were, then as weeds they would be back in no time to harass and throttle. The true ascetic labour is not an act of disintegration but of integration. It is the effort of gathering up all these feelings, emotions, endeavours and appetites, and – within the stillness of concentration upon the Divine – gradually assimilating such fleshly 'enemies' and re-directing them as a healthy, vigorous, integrated part of ourselves. It is fundamentally, the same with our own selves as what we are told to do with others: 'love our enemies'. The quest for holiness is not disintegration of self, but integration; this integration the Saints have longed for and sought throughout the centuries.

RECOGNITION OF SAINTS

How then do we recognize a saint? How have saints been recognized in the past, consciously or unconsciously? What are the signs of sainthood, if any, common to all nations and all generations? What unites St Cuthbert of north-east England with St Seraphim of Russia? Or St Mary of Egypt with a priest in a concentration camp? Where lies the innermost kernel of the unity of holiness?

The holy bond which knits together the far-flung souls of saints surely lies in the unification wherein so much that has fallen away is re-integrated, the nearest to wholeness that seems possible for a human being to achieve since the Fall. Sanctification comes step by step with the inner healing of the torn wrenching apart, the violent split of self-interest in the disintegration of disobedience.

Such growth of healing unification manifests itself, strangely enough, in much the same manner from country to country and from generation to generation. Again and again it is associated with a variety of forms of reconciliation to nature – to trees, plants, climate, the enduring of heat and cold; the eating of noxious weeds without ill effect; friendship with wild animals, docile at the feet of the Saint. Hunger ceases to trouble. Thirst parches no longer. All that 'fallen' man has gradually learned as essential to his life no longer obtains in such a state of holiness, whatever the physical agony during the time of growth. The Saint, in the final stages of life, reveals to us a hint of Paradise that used to be, and a promise of the Paradise that once more will be ours. The lives of the Saints throughout the world and throughout generations are so alike, simply because one and all they proclaim that the laws of fallen man may yet be overcome by holiness. So lions were tame in the arena.

ST CUTHBERT OF LINDISFARNE

The strange universality of holiness is brought out graciously in John Tavener's *Ikon of St Cuthbert*. Here, contained within the conventional symmetry of the Orthodox Matins Canon, together with the familiar repetition of the invocation to the Saint to pray for us sinners, comes the life of a truly great Saint of the Western world. The Ikon of St Cuthbert is a fusion of traditions at a point just beyond everyday experience: the point of holiness is no longer circumscribed by caste or creed.

The life of St Cuthbert, as told by St Bede, followed a traditional pattern: born about 634, he showed unusual signs of piety from the earliest youth; in 651 he became a monk; in Ripon, as Guest Master, he entertained an angel who came to check his rectitude; as Prior at Melrose he performed his duties zealously, teaching both monks and lay people in outlying villages; later, as Prior at Lindisfarne, he intensified his life of austerity and prayer, keeping vigil for whole nights, sometimes praying in the sea up to his neck in water; a brother witnessed two otters asking his blessing.

But, as with all ascetics throughout time and place, St Cuthbert yearned for more and more solitude. The incredible hunger for unified concentration led him to the island of Farne where he built himself a hut, drew water from the dry ground, sowed barley on barren land, and even converted two crows from stealing his thatch! The ascetic must work with his hands. The Fall may not be denied but, for the holy man, nature, as it were, gives a helping hand, a promise of the new Paradise. And so the sea helped St Cuthbert and presented him with essential timber for building.

Of course, St Cuthbert was not left in peace, nor would he wish it, however much he might long for it. The Communion of Saints does not allow for personal salvation to the exclusion of others, and the Saint cannot erode the greatest commandment of all: to love. It is not for the Saint to shut himself away from suffering humanity, even if he may do so for a short time of preparation. He must, ultimately, be open to every call upon him, every demand, justifiable or otherwise – the Saint has learned not to judge. Many people travelled long distances to St Cuthbert to seek bodily and spiritual healing. Already in his lifetime he performed many miracles, the outward seal of sanctity, even from a distance. The Abbess Elfleda was healed by a touch of his linen girdle.

Nor did St Cuthbert escape the fate of reverence and respect: he was forced to accept consecration as bishop and obediently fulfilled his episcopal duties until the time when he foresaw his own death and returned to his solitude, to die on 20 March 687. After various vicissitudes, his uncorrupt body found its final rest by 999 in Durham. In traditional form, hagiography presents the life of St Cuthbert of Lindisfarne, and so too the *Ikon of St Cuthbert*, in terms of music, recalls something of the personal fragrance, the sweet radiance of holy Father Cuthbert.

ST SERAPHIM OF SAROV

From early England to eighteenth-century Russia seems a long step; from insular Catholicism to provincial Orthodoxy seems even longer; and, yet, in the mysterious bond of holiness what could be nearer? Creatures of the sea at Cuthbert's command, beasts of the forest at Seraphim's. Another language. A rude hut not of the same material. Rocks into birch trees. People, English and Russian, intruding, demanding, sapping the last drops of human strength.

St Seraphim was born in Kursk in 1759. To our knowledge, his first vision came to him at the age of ten when he was so ill that he was expected to die. The Mother of God told him that he would be cured and live. He joined the Monastery of Sarov when he was nineteen, and once again became very ill at the age of twenty-one. Once again he was brought back to life by the vision of the Mother of God, dazzling light, the Apostles Peter and John, and the words 'He is one of ours.' At the age of twenty-eight he took his monastic vows, and in 1794 he was granted the longed-for permission to *withdraw* into the forest. The craving of the holy man throughout the centuries has been to *withdraw* from the world, if only for a time, to be alone, to be free to *listen*, to *put* all his strength into *attention*: the focusing of mind into the very heartbeat of unified direction. Yet he remained a man, and as man he humbly accepted the need for refreshment, returning to the monastery for Sundays and feasts, and then once again seeking his solitude, to share the bread he brought with the wild beasts and birds of the forest.

Yes, he was alone. Bliss? It is not as easily won. What better prey for the devil than a man, alone, defenceless, no other human being to strengthen and uphold, no one and nothing to direct, stripped of all spiritual, moral, mundane diversion? Now: seize him! Now: rend him! Now: show him the madness of his choice! Terrify him! Fling his body about! Mock him! Drag down his God! Pour filth on his cries for help! Yet Seraphim survived. Slowly, tenderly, the fragrance of Paradise replaced the fiendish stench. As steel refined, St Seraphim emerged to face the world – robbers and pilgrims. In the monastery, once again, finally, he opened his cell door.

'Freely you have received: freely give.'

'Lord Jesus Christ, Son of God, have mercy upon me a sinner.'

The Ikon of St Cuthbert, *The Ikon of St Seraphim*, are images in music of the direct impact of holiness. And how does St Mary of Egypt fit into this pattern?

ST MARY OF EGYPT

The holiness of St Mary of Egypt confronts us with a judgement on judgement. It reiterates to a point of anguish the impossibility of judging, that is, of seeing as if we can see with God's eyes. Her life is not only an obvious ascetic triumph, a triumph of love, but also a triumph over any preconceived notions of holiness. The essential message of St Mary's life would seem to reiterate the constant message of the Gospel: the abiding conviction that we do not know, nor are we meant to know, into the Mind of God and hence we cannot judge God's values.

Priest-monk Zossima was a good man. He served faithfully as a monk, performing all his duties in exemplary fashion, and he did nothing that he should not do. And yet something niggled within him. Surely there might be a greater ascetic trial for him to achieve? He could, according to his own estimation, achieve little more in his present monastery, where he had lived most of his life, so he determined to penetrate further into the desert, to a more isolated, austere monastery and see what he could learn, or rather achieve, there, for he still thought in terms of spiritual achievement. So he set out, and found his way across the Jordan to a desert monastery where the monks were well tried in ascetic labour, and where he could strive to follow their example. Yet, deep within him, the secret longing persisted: a hole, as it were, within his soul, through which all that he did fell away . . . fell . . . and was lost.

As for St Mary, what was she doing? Dancing, singing lewd songs, prostituting her body, corrupting the young men of Egypt; drinking, eating: forcing her body on all who came her way, but ever refusing payment. She earned by spinning.

From Cairo to Jerusalem – her avowed purpose was to corrupt the young men on pilgrimage for the feast of the Holy Cross. And she managed admirably. Curiosity led her to the Church, and curiosity to follow the crowd to look upon the true

Cross brought forth to the people. But violently an unseen force prevented even a glimpse: the crowd surged forward and she was repelled. Distraught, bewildered, she was overpowered by a yearning beyond all desire, and alone, rejected, she prayed to the Mother of God. She gave her whole life to Christ, our God, and the force which had repelled her, now carried her forward, forward to the Cross, forward to the Jordan, forward into the desert, forward into year after year of icy cold and burning heat, of devilish temptation, of carnal longing, of despair, and, finally, of the peace beyond all understanding.

Priest-monk Zossima and Holy Mary of Egypt met in the desert. In John Tavener's *Bless* duet, we hear the utmost humility as each begs the other for a blessing. Is he not a priest? Is she not what has eluded him all these years, the embodiment of true holiness? Mutual recognition. Redeeming love.

The story of St Mary and St Zossima is the story of 'seeming-vice' and 'seeming-virtue', the emphatic avowal that we human beings cannot judge. And we see the mercy of God who allowed the apparently parallel lines to meet before it was too late for Father Zossima. It is no accident that, faced with the Saint's dead body in the bare desert, and her written command to bury her, Father Zossima found only one source of help: a big lion, who showed every sign of friendliness and dug out with its front paws a hole big enough to bury the body. Nature redeemed: let the animals in merry dance remind us again and again that we may not judge.

THE AKATHIST

It seems fitting to end these few thoughts on holiness with the faith of a man enclosed within the grey horror of a concentration camp. Even as St John Chrysostom, dragged to his death, thanked God for all things, so this unnamed priest wrote his hymn of gratitude and praise – gratitude for all that he could no longer see or hear or smell other than in his memory with the senses of his loving, undaunted spirit. He renounces himself before all that God has created:

Glory to God for all things.

Psalms

I remember many years ago, before I was a nun, being asked by a little girl how many Psalms there were in the Bible. To my shame I had to look it up for her! Sometimes now, particularly during Lent when we say the Psalter twice a week, I look back on that incident and regret the lost years.

It is a common fallacy amongst the Orthodox that the Old Testament is somehow designed more for Protestants! How can we think this with our repeated Old Testament readings in Vigils, and Psalms in every Office, I really do not know, but it is one of those erroneous ways in which the Church divides itself even more than could be considered justifiable.

MOTHER MARIA'S TRANSLATION OF THE PSALMS

In the late 1960s, Mother Maria embarked on a voyage of translation. She set out to journey through the Psalms, which she loved, and after years of hard work on her part we published her translation in 1973. In the Preface, she writes:

> Could it not be that each Psalm had a face, a personal face, a particular, unique life, which had remained hidden from me within the eternity flow of liturgical prayer? . . . Had not every Psalm a mind? . . . *The Joy of the Law* . . . the Law as a Covenant of love between God and his people . . .

So Mother Maria set out to translate from inside the text 'as an explorer with joy and trembling, on to the vast sea of the Hebrew Psalms'. And, in her translation, I first met and experienced some of the living faith, the reality of the Psalms. The Psalms came to life, they made sense on every level; more than sense, they provoked thought, they demanded attention, they were, in fact, alive: emotions as recognizable as one's own, fears akin, shameful anger, wild spurts of longing for revenge, humble pleading, even rare moments of gratitude. They were no longer something to be chanted monotonously, now they thrilled the nerves in eager response, in the delight of recognition.

Mother Maria writes:

'Daily we rise with the Psalms, and, imperceptibly, inside the call of Christ, they lead us to look at ourselves, and into the way of repentance . . . I saw how Christ fulfilled the Psalms, as He had fulfilled the Law to its primal beauty, when he lifted the reward out of the earthly into the heavenly realm . . .'

PSALM 50 (51) (VIGIL SERVICE)

Have mercy upon me, O God,
In your goodness and love,
In your tender compassion
Wipe my sins away.
Wash me from every stain,
From my sins make me pure.
For my sin, I know it well,
My fault is unceasingly with me.

No evasion here. What could be more direct than the opening lines – the acknowledgement of sin, the personal confession, the realization that God alone can remedy such corruption – confession and plea for absolution.

Against you, you alone,
I have sinned,
That which in your eyes
Is evil, I did.

So you are just
In your sentence,
Without reproach
When you judge.

Confession of sin against God, not man, and full acceptance of judgement to follow. Further clear-sighted self-abasement:

See, I am born evil,
As a sinner my mother conceived me.

So alien to the divine intention:

But you love steadfast truth
In the inmost being.

Now comes the abrupt reversal – man debased and filthy; God pure and true. Filth, purity: can any hope remain? Yes indeed, the highest hope! The hope of divine pity:

Secretly teach me your wisdom,
With hyssop free me from sin,
And I shall be clean,
Wash me, and I shall shine
Brighter than snow.

Give me back joy and jubilation
That those bones may dance,
Which you have crushed.
Turn away your face
From my sins,
Blot out my guilt.

What a promise! What a hope! God will not only forgive but will erase the guilt. The guilt will be as if it had never been. But, no room for self-pride, no time for complacence, no space for resting in the false peace of absolution. The devils like a nice clean room to which they can return. Spiritual cleansing is no herald of rest but the call to work, urgent striving so that the foot may not slither backwards, striving with the Spirit of Life against the assaults of the spirits of death:

O God, create for me a pure heart,
Give me a new spirit,
A steadfast mind.
Do not drive me from your face,

Take not away
Your holy spirit from me.

And, if blessed, then we too should bless. God's gifts to us are not just for hoarding but for scattering prodigally abroad that all may have a share:

Restore to me
The jubilee of your help;
Give me a generous heart,
I will show to the sinners your way
That the straying come back to you.

And, from vile sin, from fear, from devils, even from good works, the road turns to the work of works – the loving praise of the Almighty:

Deliver me from bloodshed,
O God, my helper,
And my tongue shall sing
Your fair justice.
O Lord, open my lips
And my mouth shall proclaim your praise.

Yes, indeed! What gift can we offer to the Creator of all? But, in his loving kindness, He will accept our love:

My offering is a broken spirit.
A heart brought low
You will not despise.

Only then, only when we repent, only when we give all the love of our hearts, then, and only then, He will accept our sacrifices. Works without love are meaningless:

Then you shall be pleased
With righteous sacrifices,
Then young bulls shall be offered
On your altars again.

PSALM 103 (104)

If Psalm 50 (51) is a hymn in praise of the Mystery of God's love, then Psalm 103 (104) is a hymn of wonder at God's creation. All we behold is His, and all is within His tender concern.

Introduction (Verse 1)

Bless the Lord, my heart,
Lord, my God, you are great,
Covered with light as a robe.

A haunting, longing, yearning of love for the unattainable Divine. A lifting up of the soul in adoration – human worship, awe before Divine Majesty.

1 (Verses 2-4)

You spread the heavens like a tent,
On the waters you build
Your lofty rooms.
Clouds are your chariot,
You ride on the wings of the storm,
You make the winds your messengers,
The flaming fire your servant.

You founded the earth on its columns,
Unshaken for ever.
With the primeval ocean you clothed it
As with a garment,
Its waters covered the mountains.

At your threats they withdrew,
At the call of your thunder they fled,
They cleave the mountains
And wind through the valleys
To the place you have set them.
You have set for them a frontier
Which they may not surpass,
That never again should they return
To cover the earth.

The actual acts of creation are specified: nature used for this 'workman' – the skies, the land and the oceans are created and given their appointed place: they sing of the harmony and the discipline of creation, the breath of Creation. With its breath the moving Spirit brings order out of chaos and the love that inspires this disciplined order: Gratitude for the Creation which brings harmony into the warring elements of disharmony.

II (Verses 5-6)

In the gorges you call forth springs,
They make their way through the mountains,
Give to drink all the beasts of the field,
In them the wild asses quench their thirst,
The bird of the air dwells at their side,
Under the leaves of the foliage it sings.

From your lofty rooms
You give the mountains to drink,
The earth drinks its fill
Of the fruit of your sky.

Here is provision of water and food for animals out of divine love for all His creation: beasts and birds. Quite a wild sound – untamed brutes, flying birds, bird song, braying of asses, stamping of hooves, lapping of water, trickling springs: life abounding in beast, bird, and nature.

III (Verse 7)

You grow grass for the cattle,
Herbs for the use of man,
That they may raise bread from the earth,
And wine which rejoices man's heart,
That their faces may shine with oil
And bread strengthen their heart.

And now here is provision for human beings – essential food: *bread*. But also, for man's delectation, wine and oil. God provides bountifully: in His love what is both essential and what is 'luxury'. Initially, men were savage but they grew more civilized with husbandry: mourning and merry-making: not simple animal eating and drinking to sustain life.

IV (Verses 8-10)

The trees of the Lord drink their fill,
The cedars of Lebanon which he has planted.
There the sparrows build their nest,
On the top the stork has her home.
To the chamois belong the high hills,
In the rocks badgers hide.

You have set the moon
To mark the times,
The sun knows its setting,
You spread darkness
And it is night.
All the beasts of the forest stir now,
The young lions roar after prey,
Demanding of God their food.

The sun rises and they draw back,
They go to sleep in their dens
And man sets out for his work
And labours till evening comes.

A peak of the order of the universe! All is there – nature, birds, animals, man.
Everything has its part to play: to be food, to provide food, to divide the day from
the night. Chaos is now an ordered creation. Every part of creation has its individual
significance, its duty. God, the Creator, *cares* for each part: the paradox of unity
in singularity. And the voice of the Spirit persists – the bread of life.

V (Verses 11-13)

How many are your works, Lord,
Each one wisely disposed,
The earth is full of your riches.

There is the great ocean
With its big arms,
A stirring in it of fishes,
Small and great, without number.
Leviathan, whom you made
As a toy for yourself.

All these hope in you
That you would give them
Food in due time.
You give, eagerly they gather it up,
You open your hand,
They eat their fill.

The psalm returns to the theme of the opening, to human praise and worship, awe and reverence before God's mightiness and generosity. And God in his tender condescension even creates a whale – for fun! All creation turns to God in gratitude. Integration of humour.

VI (Verse 14)
But when you hide your face
They take fright,
When you recall their breath
They must die, return to their dust.
You send out your breath,
They are created,
Thus you renew
The face of the earth.

Once again, the reminder of the work of the Spirit, of the Creator: God alone breathes in life, God alone takes life, and God alone gives life again. Awesome, majestic, wind of life, sweeping all away: destruction. Then renewal. Gusts – angry. Gusts: gentle. Gusts to destroy. Gusts to give birth.

VII (Verse 15)
For ever be the glory of the Lord,
May the Lord rejoice in his works.
He looks at the earth
And it trembles,
He touches the mountains
And they smoke.

The *glory* of God in all the diversity of physical manifestations: the royalty of God, and the joy of God in what *He* has created. He loves the work of His hands.

VII (Verses 16-18)
I will sing to the Lord
As long as I live,
I will play for my God
All my days.
May my song please him,
I have my joy in the Lord.
O that sinners
Would vanish from the earth,
And the wicked be seen no more.

Bless the Lord my heart.

The human 'summing up' of devotion: worship, prayer, the promise of a life devoted to prayer and the yearning for the ultimate Theophany when evil will finally be overcome.

The Psalm ends even as it began: the lifting up of the soul in adoration. The end – the beginning. Unceasing prayer.

Psalm 136 (137)
By the rivers of Babylon
We sat and wept,
Remembering Sion.
On the willows around
We hung up our harps.

There our captors
Asked of us songs,
Our gaolers joy.
Sing us, they said,
A song of Sion.

How should we sing
A song of the Lord
In a strange land?
Should I ever forget you, Jerusalem,
May my right hand wither,
My tongue cleave to my gums,
If your memory dies in my heart,

If I count not Jerusalem
My highest joy.

Remember, Lord,
The day of Jerusalem
Against Edom's sons,
When they said,
Down with her, down with her,
Down to the ground.
Daughter of Babylon,
Blessed he who rewards you
For the evil you have done to us,
Blessed, who seizes your children
And dashes them at the rock.

Water and willows and harps: captives, gaolers: sadness of exile: glories past: single hope of revenge.

The Jews: dragged as captives to the fertile land of Babylon. Their tears watered their memories. Sion, the holy mountain of God, would not be forgotten. But had God forgotten them? Whatever else, they would not prove traitors. Their hymns would not be sung to entertain their captors. Their faith is mighty indeed. Jerusalem persists their highest joy. The desolate city one day will be rebuilt. The captive Jews, as yet without the strength of the Incarnate Word which upheld the Christian martyrs, could yet so challenge the pagan enemy with undaunted faith:

Blessed, who seizes *your* children
And dashes *them* at the rock.

How can we, as Christians, pray such overt words of violent revenge? The rock was surely no symbol, no metaphor. We can see a real rock, real captors, real prisoners; there are the babies torn from their mothers' arms, dashed against the blood-stained stone. The persecution was real: the wild wailing of forlorn motherhood. The cruelty of exile was real and so too the cry for vengeance was real. How may we deny the reality? Can we not, for one instant, share in the agony, the longing for retribution, of all the persecuted peoples of the world? Go down into the pit with them? Must we stand aloof in self-righteousness?

But, even as the Jews in Babylon, we need not stay within the desolation. The cry of the Jews was no mere cry for revenge: far more, it was a vision of faith. At the very moment of foul murder, the faith is there, already the vision of retribution. This vision of vengeance is no boast for themselves but the claim for the abiding presence of God there and then, at the vilest moment of despair. God has not deserted them. The belief in vengeance is the vindication of their faith.

Blessed he who rewards you.

The vengeance will be Divine, not human. God IS. Not only in Jerusalem but so too in Babylon: despair into worship.

If we look at this cry for vengeance in the light of victory of faith, it is no far journey to 'Blessed are they which are persecuted for righteousness' sake, for theirs is the kingdom of heaven.' Babylon may travel to the New Jerusalem.

III

The Mind

Is it not strange how difficult it is to define the mind? We may say, 'What's in your mind?' or 'Your mind's just not working', or 'My mind feels confused'. Constantly we speak of the mind. Every action we take is the outcome of the work of the mind. We might say 'That was a thoughtless thing to do', but what we mean is that a particular way of thinking led to trouble: heedless we may well be, thoughtless we cannot be.

Degrees of intelligence may certainly vary. The capacity for rational thinking is not the same from one person to another. But our minds, if nothing else, remain as long as we are alive, and are sensible to pain or pleasure in whatsoever degree of experience. Our minds, the gift of logical and conscious appraisal, bestow upon us our human pre-eminence over all other created animals.

THE LIMITATION OF THE HUMAN MIND

Yes, we may well glory in our minds, triumphant over all the rest of creation, the seas and the fish, the air and the birds, forests and beasts. We may rejoice at our great capacity for learning, for delving into the depths of the waters, the heights of the skies: we have conquered nature again and again, we have written great books, we can speak many languages. Yes, we are a wonderful human race. But, these minds of ours – all these grand things which they encompass – remain what they are: material.

We cannot think *beyond* matter: we cannot think beyond the limitations of creation. Creation may open deeper, wider, higher for us at the bidding of scientific research, it may split into many, many parts. Yet, it remains creation and with our created minds we cannot see beyond it: we cannot see *beyond* ourselves. We are *created* beings: our minds are *created*: we remain *finite*.

THE HUMAN MIND AND GOD

I think it cannot be reiterated enough that we can never see into the Mind of God. This thought is surely the great bulwark against the Satanic pride to which we are all inclined, particularly when we are making amazing scientific and mechanical discoveries or disturbing the centuries-long structure of the Christian Church. Yet, into the Mind of God, God the Creator, we cannot even have a glimpse. This is the great condescending love of the Incarnation, that we might see God within this limitation of our human capacity.

If our minds were capable of seeing beyond the finite, there would have been no need for the Incarnation, and no need for Pentecost. Hence, our limitation is also our possibility for repentance and forgiveness for the presumption of the Fall in the coming of our Lord and Saviour Jesus Christ. The Fall, put at its simplest, was the devil's suggestion to Eve, a suggestion more and more frequently repeated, a suggestion that her mind need not be humanly limited, or even constrained by Divine injunction. Strangely enough, we still manage to fall for the same delusion at every possibility! Too often we believe that we can see into the divine Mind, and that it is even our duty to re-order and re-fashion according to what seems reasonable or generous to us. At the other extreme, we condemn out of hand what does not please us, quoting the Scriptures as justification. Between such rocks we cannot but founder, and again and again we can only cry out in repentance and beg for forgiveness and mercy.

FAITH AND DOUBT

Once we accept the limitation of our minds, doubt loses its terror. Our minds cannot hold the Divine: hence we can only accept the Divine by *faith*. The doubt is unavoidable because there can be no certainty, such as the certainty about tables and chairs in the room, over the Incomprehensible. This doubt is neither sinful nor evil but an inescapable part of human limitation. Without this doubt there can be no faith. Faith is accepting the limitation of knowledge, hence accepting the doubt, accepting that the doubt paradoxically 'proves' the Divinity, and, without overcoming the doubt, persisting in the belief. Faith is *not* knowledge. Thus, when we are torn by doubt, we cry out for faith, and with this cry we are already dealing with the doubt. It cannot be dispelled in this world, but it can be endured by faith. Doubt, to put it bluntly, is the direct result of the Fall. We ceased to see God face to face, but hid our nakedness from His presence.

REPENTANCE

We love the thief on the cross very much. He was given the promise of promises: that he would enter Paradise together with Christ, the Paradise from which we had been expelled. Now the thief did not say that he had killed or stolen: to confess one's sins is the first step in repentance. Yet repentance, itself, is not being sorry – it is a persisting, active condition of the spirit, it is the yearning to be with Christ, a yearning that was satisfied for the thief on the cross, and (what is more) it is a yearning that springs from the recognition of Christ. Repentance is a confession of faith; it is an attitude of the spirit, of the mind. Repentance sees oneself as one is, sees one's own fragility, one's own weakness, one's own inadequacy, one's own limitation on every level, and turns to the One Illimitable with the plea to be remembered.

It is this plea, this contrition of the mind, which was shown to be acceptable at the very last minute possible, at the point of death. This was the greatness of the thief: he recognized God. This is the repentance for which we yearn from day to day: to see ourselves in perspective. We cannot see God, but He can see us. 'Verily I say unto thee, today shalt thou be with me in Paradise' (Luke 23:43).

THE HOLY SPIRIT

We are sometimes confused on the whole age-long controversial question of thinking, of the use of the mind. Throughout the centuries, East and West, there has always been a tendency amongst religious people to denigrate thinking, as if thinking were an enemy of the Spirit. This tendency has been particularly strong in all forms of monasticism. Monks have even gone so far as to consider that in denying themselves space for thinking they have opened themselves more directly to the unhindered communication of the Holy Spirit. This policy is dangerous, for in closing the conscious working of the mind they are weakening their defences, and while attempting to deny temptation, they are excluding the one great defence: a mind open to the influence of the Spirit.

It is neither safe nor fruitful to seek to deny our minds. In fact it is not possible. However we wriggle about, we can only ever deny thought by thinking we deny it. So it would seem safer and more fruitful, instead of fighting the inevitable, to set about seeking to train our minds, to discipline them, gradually to learn to avoid self-indulgent speculation and idle dreaming.

Once we accept positively the inevitability of thought, we can begin to learn to direct our minds carefully and lovingly to the search for Truth in every sphere: from washing dishes as true to the need of the dishes, to listening to a particular woman's marriage problems as her specifically unique burden. We should gradually learn to avoid misleading side-roads, and steel ourselves in our quest for Truth from feeling we should answer questions which are wrongly put. Such 'wrong' questions are the most difficult assaults on the mind, whether they come from others or whether they well up inside ourselves. Here I find that the Parable of the Good Samaritan is my greatest comfort – whenever I feel that I am being drawn into a wrong question, I try to stop myself from being drawn into a wrong answer by remembering the lawyer and his question.

THE QUESTION AND THE ANSWER OF THE GOOD SAMARITAN

The lawyer may have wanted to catch Christ. Secretly he may have hoped that Christ was the Saviour but, whatever the circumstances, he asked Christ what he should do to inherit eternal life. He received the sharp reply that he should know from the Law:

> Thou shalt love the Lord thy God with all thy heart, and with all thy soul, and with all thy strength, and with all thy mind; and thy neighbour as thyself.

This was the crux of the duel. Sharply the lawyer demanded, 'Who is my neighbour?' Cannot we all imagine how we should have fallen into that trap of a question wrongly put? We should have plunged into a morass of social work, of stories of the poor and needy, the sick, the Third World, and in the end we should have been left with the despairingly wide expanse of moral obligation and no spiritual test whatsoever.

'Who is my neighbour?' A reasonable and enticing question but not the immediate issue. 'Love your neighbour as yourself.' But the mind of our Saviour was filled with the light of the Spirit, and immediately He told the Parable of the Good Samaritan.

What has happened? The burden has shifted from the recipient to the donor: the *worthiness* of the victim has become irrelevant, and what has emerged is the worthiness of the *rescuer*. The question was wrongly put but answered *rightly*. Who is my neighbour? In the realm of the spirit that is not the point: No, rather, who was the neighbour to the wounded man? Love your neighbour as yourself – you do not choose your neighbour. The neighbour is you. And the lawyer, because he had a mind, understood and repented. If a man loves, then mountains will be removed and a Samaritan tenderly probe the festering wounds of a Jew.

THE HOLY SPIRIT

We cannot see God. We cannot grasp God, but He can see us and He can inspire us. The Spirit can, and surely does, visit us, not only sacramentally, not only when we are praying, but also when we are trying to think clearly and honestly. Surely our greatest human thoughts come with the breath of inspiration. We must work with them, lose them, find them again, give them form or shape in verse or music or philosophy. When the Spirit is missing, the truth also lacks: that particular recognition, when creating something, that no word, no note, no line could be altered, suggests the presence of the Spirit. What we may call a work of genius is inevitably recognized by the inevitability of every detail in the particular work.

As far as our own creative efforts are concerned the Spirit certainly inspires us to the Truth. But here we come to a particularly important theological concept, more important today perhaps than at any other time.

The Divine is eternal, there is no time, no beginning, no end. The Divine is outside time – what was, and is, and shall be. The Holy Spirit does not provide us with 'new' ideas concerning God from century to century: the Gospels revealed God to us within time once and for all in His self-limitation. For our faith and our religious practice the Gospels are foundation and edifice. The Divine is not concerned with the passing of time, nor should our religion be affected by time or fashion. The Spirit renews, makes fresh, reminds, keeps alive whatever is from the beginning and the Spirit does so, not as the instrument of temporal changes, but as the persistent reminder that no passing of time should touch what is outside time, namely our Christian faith. The Spirit does not innovate. We change. We have aeroplanes instead of horses, antibiotics instead of herbs. But, how devastating it would be if the Divine followed our transitory moods! If the Divine were not Eternal, Immutable, Incomprehensible! The Holy Spirit is our salvation against mortal change: the Spirit retains the unchanging Truth in the face of a transitory world. The Spirit is our safeguard against all that would undermine the Faith.

TRADITION AND TRADITION

We hold fast to the concept of Tradition as a bulwark of faith, and, in effect, the Rock on which alone we balance in some degree of safety. Tradition: in the early years of the Church, when the Church was as yet unbroken by internal strife, the Faith, under the inspiration of the Holy Spirit, was laid down in Creed and Canons. The Faith was handed down to the Church over the centuries by Tradition from the Apostles and the earliest days: from Christ God Himself, and it is our constant prayer that we may not transgress this Tradition. We pray to the Holy Spirit ever to help and inspire us that the Tradition may be kept alive in our hearts and minds and lives, for we believe that what we have inherited is the true faith given to the Church by Christ, our God. This for us is the work of the Holy Spirit, to be our protection against changing fashions, novel ideas, contemporary demands. He is our guard against the idolatry of the world. He inspires us with eternal Truth, untouched by transient human taste. Fallible, sinful, stupid as we are, we believe that we have at least some measure of safety if we pray to the Holy Spirit to renew ever and again what has been passed on to us by the Tradition of the Church. What else is the meaning of Pentecost?

But, here, I feel I should give a word of warning on mere tradition or custom. This should never be identified with Tradition, nor indeed with faith, and I fear that we in the Orthodox Church are somewhat inclined to this mild but nonetheless exclusive form of idolatry! It varies from country to country. Easter would not be Easter for the Russians without pascha (a form of cream cheese) and kulich (a form of sweet bread). Coloured eggs are highly important. In Greece on Holy Friday, women spend hours and hours arranging flowers for the shroud. At the Feast of the Transfiguration, grapes are essential as first fruit. And so it goes on: all warm and loving and significant but not to be taken too seriously and certainly not meant to figure as an essential part of Orthodoxy.

Tradition and tradition: Tradition the backbone of our faith, tradition a sweet savour.

But, whatever else, we pray that the Holy Spirit will ever come down on us, not for change, but for renewal of the faith which was, and is, and shall be.

King of Heaven, Comforter, Spirit of Truth, everywhere present and filling all things, treasure of blessings and giver of life, come and abide in us, cleanse us from all corruption, and of your goodness save our souls (Pentecost *Hymn to the Holy Spirit*).

IV

Ikons

I am a little diffident on the question of embarking upon the subject of ikons because, as so many old Orthodox, I am, to put it mildly, somewhat 'touchy' on the subject. Nothing irritates me more than being told brightly or earnestly by visitors that they do love ikons, or that they have such a lovely ikon, or, worst of all, that they are learning to paint ikons, or even worse than the worst, that they are teaching others to paint them! So, perhaps, just for once, I should like to take a deep breath and say something of what ikons really mean to us. If I am somewhat harsh and exclusive in my pronouncements I beg to be forgiven, for it is difficult for a tiny minority to keep its integrity of faith.

ORIGIN OF IKONS

According to Tradition, the origin of ikons is a gracious story. Avgar (or Abgar), king of a province in Mesopotamia, entered into correspondence with our Lord, Jesus Christ. Avgar begged our Lord to come and heal him from a severe sickness, assuring Him of his faith in His divinity. King Avgar not only invited the Saviour to his city of Edessa, but offered to divide his kingdom with Him (Satan's temptation lovingly echoed!) Christ refused the invitation, telling Avgar that His mission on earth was nearing completion. Avgar, undaunted, then sent his royal artist to paint the likeness of Christ, but the artist was unable to fulfil his task because he was dazzled by the brilliance of the divine countenance. In His mercy, however, the Lord took pity on such persistent importunity, as He so frequently did in His earthly ministry, and taking a piece of linen, or a handkerchief, placed it against His face: miraculously, the outline of the divine countenance was traced on the cloth: this is believed to be the first ikon, *not made by hand*.

It is this likeness, however derived, we find in all authentic Ikons of Christ. Thus, traditionally, Ikons were not only countenanced and blessed by our Lord, but the first one was, in fact, made by Him, and of Him. Whether or not this story is true in the historical sense, or in the practical meaning of truth, the fact remains in its essential veracity that we venerate Ikons as the *representation of the reality*, the imprint on the linen of the actuality refused to Avgar. But, because they are *not* the reality, we do not worship them, nor accord to them the reality denied to Avgar.

WHAT IKONS ARE NOT

I am so often asked what Ikons are, or told what they are thought to be, that, for once, I should like to start with the negative:

Ikons are NOT works of art.
Ikons are NOT realistic.
Ikons are NOT in accordance with individual creativity.
Ikons are NOT holy pictures.
Ikons are NOT religious greeting cards.
Ikons are NOT objects of superstition (NOT good luck charms in motor cars).

To sum up: ikons are not what they are not.

WHAT ARE IKONS?

It is always much easier, particularly for the Orthodox, to say what things are NOT, rather than what they are, presumably because we hold so fast to the reality of the ultimate Mystery that we have difficulty in giving constricting outlines even in the initial stages of definition. Whatever is connected with the spiritual, in whatever sphere, always has the unattainable and incomprehensible proportion that is beyond our finite comprehension. As ever, we can only touch the hem of the garment – but that was enough for the faithful woman and surely should be sufficient for us. Yes, as the years go on, we certainly can do more and more with the atom, but understanding an Ikon is another matter – and it must be approached in another way.

Ikons are an integral part of the Orthodox faith. They are not an artistic adornment, or an aid to prayer according to personal taste, or any form of private devotion. When I insist that they are an integral part, I mean, without even considering the role of individual ikons, that the very existence of Ikons is dogmatic. Ikons keep the fact of the Incarnation alive for us: Christ, in His tender love for humanity, took upon himself a human form, real flesh and blood, so that the memory of His hands, His feet, His side, could stay with us unto the ages of ages. No wonder the Holy Apostle Thomas was blessed.

So too the Ikons continue for us the immediate promise of the Incarnation. Christ was there, flesh and blood, and the Ikon, as we believe in some form once blessed by Him, constantly reminds us of His actual presence. He and His holy ones, His Mother, His saints, are with us now, in person, and ever will be. And the Ikons not only keep the memory alive, but, by divine grace, hold within them the living holiness: Christ now, His Mother now, His saints now. Christianity is not a religion based on something that happened in the past. Christianity is present. And to help our faith in this, we are surrounded by the Mystery of the Ikons: wood and paint, and yet not wood and paint.

However, human beings are inclined to idolatry and superstition. To prevent this where Ikons are concerned, the Church has preserved over the centuries the purity of the stylized Ikon. Nothing is permitted that might allow a realism that could lead us to forget that Ikons only *represent*: *they* are not. This is why statues are forbidden, as is anything 'natural' that might confuse the medium with the Truth *within* the medium. Thus Ikons should not only be stylized in execution but they should also be without any touch of personal artistic deviation from tradition. The line between veneration and idolatry is very fine; hence the tradition of Ikon painting has been preserved and handed down within the Church from generation to generation, zealously preserved. And an Ikon, even if painted 'correctly' to the last detail, is still not an Ikon until and unless it has the blessing of the Church.

BLESSING OF IKONS

The prayers for the blessing of Ikons are not only revealing in their theological significance, they also seem to me very beautiful. Somehow these prayers take us out of this world into a realm still temporal but outside change; a realm as ageless, and yet inside the ages, as mountains and lakes and the Sea of Galilee. Very few English-speaking people know these prayers, so perhaps it might be of interest if I quote from some of them to give a 'flavour' of the particular fragrance of Ikon veneration.

From the blessing of an Ikon of Christ God:

Lord God Almighty, God of our fathers, who desires to deliver Your people, Israel the chosen, from the seduction of idol worship, and ever to hold them unswervingly in the knowledge and service of You the one true God, You forbade with punishment their making for themselves images and likenesses in opposition to You the true God . . . You ordered a sanctuary, and for two golden cherubim to be placed above the ark of testimony . . . and in Your mercy You accepted the honour paid to it as rendered to Yourself. And in the fulness of time You sent Your only begotten Son, our Lord Jesus Christ, born of a woman, ever-virgin Mary, and He took upon Himself the form of a servant and He was in the likeness of man, and He depicted the likeness of His own most pure image unmade by hands in laying the handkerchief to His most holy face . . . And so we, O Lord, God Almighty, this Ikon of Your beloved Son . . . reverently present before Your majesty, not as a graven image of God, but witnessing to the fact that veneration of the Ikon ascends to the prototype . . . look upon us mercifully and upon this Ikon and for the sake of the incarnation and manifestation of your only begotten Son in whose memory this has been made, send down on it Your heavenly blessing and the grace of the most holy Spirit, and bless and sanctify it: endue it with the power of healing, and of driving off all the wiles of the devil . . .

At the actual blessing, the priest sprinkles the Ikon with sanctified water and says:

This Ikon is sanctified by the grace of the most Holy Spirit, through the sprinkling of this sanctified water, in the name of the Father and of the Son and of the Holy Spirit.

The hymn after the blessing:

We bow down, O Good One, before Your pure Ikon, beseeching forgiveness for our transgressions, Christ God: for freely you chose of Your grace to go up on the Cross in the flesh, that You might deliver whom You created from the enemy's bondage. And so, we gratefully cry out to You: with joy You filled all things, when You came, O Saviour, to save the world.

The Ikon to be an Ikon as we understand it, must be a real Ikon, that is painted strictly within the tradition and blessed by a Priest of the Orthodox Church.

The prayers for the blessing of Ikons of Saints make a very clear distinction between the worship due to God alone, and the reverence due to His Saints:

> . . . and as we reverently venerate the representation of this Saint, we are venerating Your image . . . and thus we pray to You to send down Your blessing . . . and sanctify this Ikon unto Your glory and to the honour and memory of Your Saint . . .

A NOTE ON BEHAVIOUR

I am often surprised by the way people treat Ikons. It may help to remember that they are blessed and should therefore be treated with due reverence. When we approach to venerate Ikons in Church or at home, we should approach reverently but modestly. An over-indulgence in bowing and crossing oneself can be as distracting as ill manners; we should avoid touching the Ikon, or pointing out an interesting characteristic by a dab of the finger; we should kiss it tentatively, in the nearest corner, with the least emotional or ritualistic show possible and without any suggestion of possessiveness.

If it is necessary to transport an Ikon from one place to another, it should be wrapped in a clean cloth, and if more than one Ikon is carried at the same time they should be placed face to face. We are carrying or touching or venerating holy objects, blessed by the grace of the Holy Spirit, representing in a Mystery Christ himself, either directly or through his Saints. It is a dreadfully uncomfortable feeling when visitors poke a finger on an Ikon saying, 'What does this bit mean?'

PAPER IKONS

At first glance, this seems a contradiction in terms! After all that I have said, how can I speak of paper Ikons? I think once again I must repeat that we do not worship our Ikons. We respect them, we love them, we venerate them, we pray before them but not to them: we pray through them to Him whom in His love for us we can actually see. Ikons give us the presence which the written word cannot achieve. However, England is not the home of the Orthodox faith. The Book of Common Prayer is obtainable, and Roman missals, breviaries, rosaries, and statues are available – why should there be Ikons? Only the few brought out from Orthodox countries, mainly Russian or Greek, are 'real' Ikons. But, the need is great and so, for some years now, there has been an increasingly brisk trade in 'paper ikons'. For years, as a monastery, we withstood these paper reproductions – better only a very few but real ones. Yet, finally, we surrendered our somewhat idealistic position.

Surely the grace in the real Ikon could somehow, by grace, transfer to a paper representation? Surely a good paper copy was 'better' than a poorly, improperly executed 'original', or nothing at all! And so I have come to think of paper ikons not as Ikons, but as ikons of Ikons – representations of Ikons! And, if they are loved and carefully mounted on wood and treated with due respect, they can blossom. I do draw the line at postcards or little trinkets being called Ikons. However, I cannot enter into the charity of the Almighty. Who knows what He can do in His loving kindness? I think we should try to keep some standards and leave the extremes to Him.

This may be the place for a note on Orthodox economy. I think paper ikons are a legitimate economy, but it must be remembered that economy is not another word for licence, for a moral or religious free-for-all! Economy is the day-to-day practical expression of the theological truth that nothing can be absolute in this created world. We are not allowed to see into the ultimate divine judgement, and thus the door is left open to bypass any human ruling if love suggests toleration. Our human laws must not be our masters; we rule through our laws. Hence, paper 'Ikons'.

ENRICHMENT

My last thought on Ikons is by way of a plea to my Western brothers and sisters. I hear so much talk of the necessity of their 'enriching' themselves from the Orthodox. Perhaps this is a passing fashion, but at present it is very active. They visit us, and I think they honestly believe that, if we feel anything, it must be a sense of satisfaction at being recognized and sought out. But, perhaps, these searchers after enrichment could remember that many of the Orthodox in England are either émigrés (or the children of émigrés) or refugees, that they have little in life other than their faith, and their Ikons. The glories of the Byzantine Empire, the riches, the splendour, are of the past. We are poor, Naboth's vineyard.

Tread softly, because you tread on my dreams. (Yeats)

POSTSCRIPT ON MUSIC

An Ikon is a picture, stylized, traditional in appearance, what it is and what it represents. Austere, unemotional, unromantic – a meaning within the 'story'. If extended and not contained within a strict traditional expression, an Ikon may be seen as being of the same family as a fable or allegory. *Pilgrim's Progress* could be regarded as an unorthodox, narrative Ikon. Thus, certain music is associated with

Ikons, in as much as every part of the composition has its essential place within a severe pattern of composition, with inter-relationship not only of traditional music, but also of traditional iconographic method of composition. Not a voice, not an instrument is outside the symmetry of the whole – beautiful, awesome, merry, cruel as so many colours and subjects, but all contained within the metaphor of the Ikon.

V

The Mother
of God

We are told so little of her who, with her love and her trust, opened Heaven for us. She, first of all mankind, willingly opened her door to suffering when she submitted herself to God. Listening, ever alert, with a heart wide open to God, she was ready to suffer, ready for the sword. The sword she received as simply and as willingly as she had conceived her divine Son. But at the moment when she passed through her inner death, she was made a mother in a yet wider sense. As a mother she received us all from the hands of her Lord and her Son on the Cross that she might help us in our turn gladly to open our hearts to the sword and show us how to turn it into joy.

(Mother Maria: *The Hidden Treasure*)

Yes, it is so strange how little we really know about the Mother of God and yet how much we believe, and how vast is her importance and influence on our lives. The very fact that we know so little is perhaps a clue to her significance, which wholly overflows the restricting limits of place and time.

In our prayers and hymns we use every possible and even fantastic-sounding superlative to express our love and admiration and reverence for the Mother of God: the *Theotokos:* the birth-giver of God. Not only the birth-giver of Jesus Christ, but of God: thus, from the outset, we suggest her unique importance, for she alone was the physical means of the Incarnation, she alone was chosen to give birth to God – to give God, who is beyond space or time, a defined physical shape, that we might see and worship Him in the Person of the Son. Yet, this was no imposition laid tyranically upon her. She was willing to accept this terrifying mission.

If we trace the part of the Mother of God through the relevant Feasts of the Church, we may enjoy the wealth of her gifts to mankind. Why do we love her so, trust her so? Why do we name her All-holy, Most holy, All-pure? Why is she to be more honoured that the Cherubim and the Seraphim? Who is she, who occupies but a comparatively few lines of the Gospels?

THE BIRTH OF OUR MOST HOLY LADY THE MOTHER OF GOD AND EVER-VIRGIN MARY (8 SEPTEMBER)

According to the Church calendar we keep this feast of the Birth of the Mother of God on 8 September, and the words of the Services on that day make it eminently clear that we believe it to have been a real birth: a real mother Anna, a real father Joachim. We celebrate their memory on the following day, 9 September. Above all, she was a real baby of real parents. If we should remove any one aspect of the reality of her human birth, this would detract from the unique miracle, as we believe it to be, of the birth of her divine Son.

Two hymns in particular, especially appointed to be sung on the day of her birth, reflect our love and reverence for her, but already also suggest where lies her ultimate importance.

The Apolytikion[1]

Your birth, Mother of God, proclaimed joy to all the world: for from you rose the Sun of Righteousness, Christ our God: the curse He destroyed and blessing bestowed: and vanquishing death, He granted to us eternal life.

The Kontakion[2]

Joachim and Anna were freed from the reproach of childlessness, and Adam and Eve from corruption of death, in your holy birth, Most Pure. Your people also celebrate this, delivered by it from punishment of sin, and they cry to you: the barren has borne the Mother of our God and the nourishment of our life.

The immediate cause of the *Kontakion*, the birth of Mary, passes further (as in the *Apolytikion*) to her future significance for the whole of humanity. I cannot over-emphasize the theological significance of this delicate discrimination.

She was born as a normal child, yet from infancy this baby was dedicated to the service of God: as a tiny child she was taken into the Temple by her parents to be brought up in the purity of virginity.

THE ENTRY OF THE MOTHER OF GOD INTO THE TEMPLE (21 NOVEMBER)

The Church celebrates the dedication of the child Mary at a special Feast in her honour, and the hymns of the day show all the joy of the anticipation of salvation. For with her dedication in the Temple the immediate history of our salvation begins.

The Apolytikion

Today is the preface to the good will of God, and the proclamation of man's salvation. The Virgin is clearly marked out in the Temple of God, and proclaims in advance Christ to all. And loudly we cry to her: 'Hail you who fulfil the Creator's plan!'

The *Kontakion*

The *Kontakion* maintains her importance as the primary vehicle of our salvation. In image she herself becomes the Temple containing Christ:

The most pure Temple of the Saviour, the precious bridal chamber and Virgin, the sacred treasury of the glory of God, today is brought into the House of the Lord, and brings with her the grace, that which is in the Spirit of God: it is she to whom God's Angels sing: she is the heavenly abode.

THE ANNUNCIATION (25 MARCH)

As we approach each Feast in turn of the *Theotokos*, we become more and more aware of the strictness of our theological approach towards her. We may describe her in the most exotic imagery, but we never venerate her in her own right: over and over again we are emphatically reminded that she remains the beloved but only the medium of the Divine. And when we turn from traditional sources to the indisputable reality of the Gospels, we see how precisely this moderation is conveyed in every appearance she makes.

And in the sixth month the angel Gabriel was sent from God unto a city of Galilee, named Nazareth. To a virgin espoused to a man whose name was Joseph, of the house of David; and the virgin's name was Mary (Luke 1:26-7).

These familiar words, simple narrative, undramatic, introduce the most stupendous event of human history: the Incarnation of God. And, as simple as the narrative is, so is the Virgin's response. She cannot understand how she can bear a child, for she is a virgin, but she accepts in total obedience the divine decree. She must have realized the probable consequences for herself – the scandal, the disgrace, perhaps death. But, she gives herself, in the fullness of faith:

> Behold the handmaid of the Lord; be it unto me according to thy word. And the angel departed from her.

So direct is this statement of obedience that the magnitude of the positive acceptance might well escape us. Not a word of questioning, of requiring more detail, even of seeking proof of the authenticity of the message. There was nothing more to say. The message was given – accepted – the angel left her.

The *Kontakion*

The *Kontakion* is sung throughout the year on a variety of occasions, but at the actual Feast of the Annunciation it seems to ring out in all its triumph: the young Virgin, the Conqueror of the world, she, alone, chosen to give birth to Christ God; she, to whom generation after generation can cry for help in the assurance of her compassion:

> Mighty conquering warrior Mother of God, we your servants whom you have freed from ills offer up to you songs of thanksgiving, and with your unconquerable power, deliver us from all affliction, that we may cry to you, hail bride unwedded!

THE NATIVITY OF OUR LORD AND SAVIOUR JESUS CHRIST (25 DECEMBER)

So we come, by way of her obedience, to Christmas, to the moment awaited in the history of man's salvation. The promise, the King of Kings, the Messaiah, the Deliverer of the Jews. What does it mean? What has happened to all the anticipated triumph?

To begin with, there is nothing but shock and shame. Joseph, the Betrothed, would have hidden Mary away, had not the angel of the Lord appeared to him in a dream and told him not to be afraid 'for that which is conceived in her is of the Holy Ghost.' Then came the journey to Bethlehem and the unemotional plain statement of fact in St Luke's Gospel:

And she brought forth her firstborn son . . . and laid him in a manger: because there was no room for them in the inn.

Perhaps this initial human rejection would be less awesome if St Luke had elaborated, but the very simplicity fills us with dread. It is the indifferent rejection at His birth which would culminate in the vituperative rejection at His death. The thread of Divine condescension is unbroken. Mary held God in her arms.

The *Kontakion*

Today the Virgin bears him beyond substance, and the earth offers a cave to the Unapproachable. Angels with shepherds give glory. Wise men journey with a star: for he has been born for us. A newborn child, God before the ages.

THE FEAST OF THE PRESENTATION (2 FEBRUARY)

The *Apolytikion*

Hail, full of grace, Virgin Mother of God, for from you has shone forth the Sun of Righteousness, Christ our God, giving light to those in darkness. And you, O righteous Elder, rejoice, for you have received in your arms the deliverer of our souls, who grants us resurrection.

She was spared nothing: the shock of the Annunciation, the anger of Joseph, the birth in a stable; and now when, according to custom, she presents her first-born in the Temple, her future agony is foretold: 'Yea, a sword shall pierce through thy own soul also.' It was in the pattern of her whole life of self-denial that she faithfully obeyed the Law in presenting her first-born son in the Temple; knowing, as she alone knew, who the Child was, she might well have thought it inappropriate to submit Him to the Law. But she did not question. We have much to learn from such scrupulous self-denying obedience, particularly in our own times when obedience, in any sphere, no longer goes unquestioned.

Step by step the holy Mother followed her divine Son through the unfolding of the Gospels, but she is never prominent. She is hidden somewhere with the other women, tending, serving, watching – and waiting for the inevitable catastrophe. At the most she is blessed with others who believe in Him. But the sword awaits her.

THE CROSS

> Now there stood by the cross of Jesus his mother, and his mother's sister, Mary the wife of Cleophas, and Mary Magdalene. When Jesus therefore saw his mother, and the disciple standing by, whom he loved, he said unto his mother, Woman, behold thy son! Then saith he to the disciple, Behold thy mother! And from that hour that disciple took her unto his own home (John 19:25-7).

Whenever I read these lines, I am filled with a deep sense of the immensity of the Church. I see Christ God crucified by men, but of His will and certainly not ours, conqueror not victim, and yet in all the agony of a real and cruel death. And, at the moment of this human pain, come the divine words: St John: the whole Church: and Mary, His mother. They were given to each other. St John took her into his home, and her protection would enfold him. It is a most awesome moment of the first intermingling of divine and human: a real mother: a real Son: a real new son. And yet, not as simple. No wonder we pray to the Mother of God for her protection.

THE FALLING ASLEEP OF THE MOTHER OF GOD (15 AUGUST)

Now we leave Gospel truth for what may be seen as legend; yet legend as it may well be, inside there is the kernel of faith. The facts may not be true – they have not been accepted as such – but there is, as it were, a devotional truth: allegorical or factual. *The Falling Asleep* points to an abiding belief in her purity, her place amongst the chosen disciples, and the love of her Son for her – in a way, if one could look at it so narrowly, it is a reward for her life of self-sacrifice; certainly it is a fulfilment. The Orthodox Church has no dogma of the Assumption, so we are left free not to insist on the everyday outer truth; however, the inner truth is very true for us.

The story of her falling asleep is one of the most tender expressions of the love we feel for the Mother of God, a love we inherited from the Apostles. When she knew that her death was near, the Apostles came to Jerusalem from the ends of the earth to be with her: from Rome, from Tiberias, from India, from Alexandria, from Thebes, and others came from out of their tombs. At her request, the Apostles took her body to bury her in Gethsemane:

> And when the third day was fulfilled . . . we all perceived that her spotless

and precious body was translated into paradise. (Apocryphal New Testament)

We do not ask how, but we are convinced that the Mother of God cannot be far from her Son, and we are equally sure that her love for her Son overleaps boundaries of time and space. She is our Mother to whom we turn for protection.

People often say, 'Why do you need the Saints, why do you need Mary? Surely, Christ, our Lord, is sufficient?' The only answer is 'Love is not exclusive, love widens, not narrows. If we love a father, is this a reason for not loving a husband? A mother? A wife? Of course, in one sense, Christ God is sufficient, but what does sufficient mean? And why disobey his dying behest "Behold thy mother!"?'

THE PROTECTING VEIL (1 OR 31 OCTOBER)

Now, in heaven, the Mother of God still does not forsake us, and the Feast of the Protecting Veil serves as one of the most explicit examples of her tender concern.

Constantinople in the early tenth century was filled with dread and fear of the threatened Saracen invasion. The cries of the faithful rose to heaven, and the cries were not ignored. In the church at Vlacherni, Andrew, the holy fool, together with his disciple Epiphanios, saw the Mother of God during the all-night vigil. He saw her, high above him in the air. She was surrounded by a host of saints and she was praying earnestly and holding her veil, or stole, as a shelter over the Christians. The pagan army was driven off. In times of crisis, and there have been many since then, this vision persists, and we know that whatever happens, a Mother's love is shielding us. At the worst, only our mortal bodies can defy her prayer.

A POSTSCRIPT ON IKONS OF THE MOTHER OF GOD

For those, and there are many, who cannot feel comfortable over our Orthodox love for the *Theotokos*, it may be of some interest to know that all Ikons of her must include her Child. We have no veneration of His Mother without the divine Son. We venerate her only as His Mother, not in her own right. We venerate her for all that we believe she has done, and does, and will do as His Mother through Him. But, humbly, we follow the holy Apostle John and take her into our homes, and into our hearts:

More honoured than the Cherubim, the Seraphim surpassing in glory, without stain you gave birth to God, the Word, true Mother of God, you we exalt.

1. *Apolytikion* is the name given to the short hymn dedicated to the Saint of the Feast of the day.
2. *Kontakion* is a short hymn appointed for a particular day, said or sung at appropriate points in the service.

VI

Prayer

Why is prayer such a difficult subject? Why have so many written so much about it throughout the Christian decades? Why am I so foolish as to try and say something more on this much-belaboured subject?

Study groups, exercises: private – communal; spontaneous – formal; congregational – priestly; public – secret; loud – whispered; grateful – mournful; reproachful, angry, demanding, challenging. Books and books, pleading hearts and critical minds, poetry and prose. And now I am starting again. Prayer: the universal language. Prayer: the cry of the world.

THE LORD'S PRAYER

It is the greatest of comforts that Christ's own disciples, the men constantly with Him, who knew more about Him than we can ever dream, asked the same question, made the same request, and, above all, needed the same reassurance. The request:

> And it came to pass, that, as he was praying in a certain place, when he ceased, one of his disciples said unto him, Lord, teach us to pray, as John also taught his disciples (Luke 11:1).

And so the Lord's Prayer was given to us, holding within it all that we need as a

Church, the whole Church, the Communion of Saints as one.

Our Father

I once knew a woman who, to my horror, used to pray 'My Father'. Her argument was that she could not account for anyone else but that she knew that God was her Father. Apart from the pride of such disobedience to the words given by Christ, she was doing herself dreadful harm by isolating herself from the Communion of the one Church, cutting herself off from the Saints, and leaving herself to flounder alone in the wide, wide sea of temptation. With that one word, *our,* we enter into the freedom of the whole Christian world, on earth and in heaven. We are not abandoned to icy isolation but enter into the joy of the Saints, past, present, future: we enter into a world no longer finite, bound by time and space. We are permitted by Christ himself to join in – no exclusion: our. And Father? No, not the greybeard of childish nightmares but the first Person of the Trinity. Father, Son and Holy Spirit. Three Persons, one Godhead. We pray ourselves immediately into the Mystery, and out of the greybeard, somewhere in the clouds, who punishes us for every little fault, who demands our obedience, who avenges every misdeed. Our Father: He is the first Person of the Trinity, who in His tender love for mankind shows Himself to us in the Second Person, Christ God. We cannot see the Father, but we can see the Son, God incarnate. 'I and my Father are one' (John 10:30).

Our Father: with these words we are into the very innermost heart of the Mystery of the Trinity.

In Heaven

God, the Father, is distinct from the Incarnate Son. He is in heaven, and we only see Him in his Son. Heaven? How can we define heaven, how understand it? Perhaps the negative approach may be the most vivid. Heaven is not the world as we understand it. Heaven is not limited. Heaven is not inside our intellectual scope. God the Father is beyond finite limitation and this we can only describe as heaven. Not the world – Unattainable.

May your name be hallowed

We must – it is our duty, our delight – keep the name of God holy. It is also our prayer that His name will be kept holy. Our prayer, our longing, our defiance of evil. His name is holy, whatever the assaults of the devil. We will invest His name with all the purity in our power. Whatever else corrupts, God the Father must remain apart, divine in every sense, worshipped as the Father. His name: God and Father.

Your Kingdom come

The prayer of the End. The prayer for that final Day of Judgement. The prayer that this world, as we know it, will be no more, but its place will be taken. No more time. No constriction of human limitation. The prayer of the totally unknown, of human trust, human faith. If it is the Kingdom of God, then it cannot but be wonderful, literally beyond all imagination. The yearning, the longing – in dread and in joyful anticipation: your Kingdom come. A divine Rule – No more injustice, no more persecution, no more tyranny – God in the totality of His sovereignty.

And we need the courage to pray it. We must have faith to dare to pray for the coming of this divine Kingdom. Can we face the blaze of glory? Shall we not shrivel faced with the Love? How dare we pray for the Kingdom of God? How, if at all, can we prepare for it?

Your will be done, on earth as in heaven

We can only prepare for the Day of Judgement by, as it were, living it ahead of its time. Our longing, our aim in life as Christians is the impossible: that our world should live in obedience to God, even as the angels, even as the Mother of God, even as the Saints.

Heaven, the home of God. On one level, the world is the antithesis of heaven; symbolically we look up to the sky, and in image heaven is 'up there', outside place and time. What do we really know of God's will? All that His Son has taught us and to which we hold fast in Gospel and Tradition – God's will, Christ's teaching, the Saints' practice. Your will be done on earth as in heaven – the pitiful yearning in this plea and, so too, an unearthly courage in even daring to give utterance to such a manifest impossibility.

Give us today our daily bread

There is brave trust in these words. How dare we demand sustenance from God Almighty? Yet, why should we not dare, when God Incarnate distributed those little loaves to that multitude? Yes, a demand for material food, for the necessities of life, and a demand that we dare to make because our Master taught us to make it. We have the right to ask for it boldly, openly, no polite dissimulation: give us.

Yet there is another side to it. Give us today our daily bread: is it not also a prayer of trust? We stipulate no recipe for the bread. Could it be martyrdom? Persecution? Sickness? It is a prayer of ultimate submission to the Divine Will: not a servile submission, not a passive acceptance but a positive demand. Give us today, this very day, what You desire for us. And we cannot, even if we so wished, blame God for what comes to us. We have prayed for it.

And forgive us our debts as we forgive our debtors

This follows on from the daily bread. So, somehow, the daily bread is connected with our fellow beings. Do we owe them, as it were, for the bread? Do they owe us? Certainly, as Christians, we cannot imagine ourselves alone and without responsibility in this world. Our hope lies in the next world, but while we live our work is here – and, again, in some mysterious fashion, we shall receive according to our giving.

'Freely you have received, freely give' (Matthew 10:8). There is a Divine measure for which we have no means of measurement other than blindly putting ourselves into the divine will: believing that in as much as we 'give to drink unto one of these little ones a cup of cold water only in the name of a disciple', we may pray that the reward of forgiveness may be ours. Above all, surely forgiveness is not a conscious act of pardon for this or that particular sin or misdeed. Forgiveness is for our very being, our fallen nature. And so, if we ask God to forgive us our debts of depravity to Him, so too we must have a deeply rooted change of heart towards our fellow beings. In other words, we must learn to love. Then we can say with the holy Apostle Paul '. . . ye ought rather to forgive him, and comfort him, lest perhaps such a one should be swallowed up with overmuch sorrow' (2 Corinthians 2:7).

And lead us not into temptation

Let us be humble and know our limitations of mind and of body. We are not all capable of martyrdom. How many of us can face ridicule, let alone the flames of persecuting fire? Can we face the lions? Can we face any persecution when it really affects our own well-being? There is always a valid excuse, an honestly valid excuse: financial responsibility for elderly relatives, our own young families. No one would question the importance of such duties. And so, in the agony of repentance, we pray to God that He will not choose us for the test – that He will not seek to prove the validity of our Christian faith, of our obedience to the Church founded on the Rock and ever refreshed by the Spirit. We are not only physical but moral cowards and thus in the clarity of remorse we throw ourselves before the Judgement Seat: Lead us not into temptation.

But deliver us from the evil one

Who is the Devil? A shapeless figure. We know that he dared to tempt Christ. We know that he assumes many shapes. We know that once he was an angel and can still assume a semblance of virtue. We know that we must avoid and fear him, that we must not yield to his winning words, the dreadful parody of virtue with which he might entice us. Yet we cannot control his movements: he can creep into our hearts, our minds, our very being. He can sap our strength. He can set up false images of virtue. There is very little that he cannot do. But the very little is the very great. He cannot face the Truth. He shrinks. Hence the prayer to Him who is the Truth: but deliver us from the evil one.

The Lord's Prayer of course is sufficient. It is the petition of the Church in unison of necessity. What then is the place of the Creed?

THE CREED

Where the Lord's Prayer is the daily prayer for what is essential for all of us, the Creed seems to me not so much a supplication as an affirmation of faith, a declaration of the individual positive acceptance of the dogma of the Church, derived from the Apostles, retained by Tradition, ratified and refined to the uttermost nicety of language by the Councils of the Church. When we say the Creed, each one of us asserts his deliberate and creative acceptance of the validity of church doctrine. Thus, it is no longer the plural number of the Lord's Prayer, 'Our Father', but it is singular. Sometimes it sounds to me as a war-cry – defiant, exultant. Can any human voice pronounce in greater triumph than in the battle-cry introduction to the Creed – let the trumpets sound and the drums roll to the gauntlet of those opening words:

I believe in one God, Father Almighty, maker of heaven and earth, and of all things, visible and invisible

There is no 'we'. It is I, I alone, my witness, my readiness for martyrdom, my declaration aloud to friend and foe, the final solitude of the Christian soul: I believe. Our Father, one God, Father Almighty.

And in one Lord Jesus Christ, the only-begotten Son of God, begotten of the Father before all ages: light of light, very God of very God, begotten not made, being of one substance with the Father, by whom all things were made.

The First Person of the Trinity: the Father. And the Second Person of the Trinity: the Son. The fine distinction for which no mortal words are adequate: Begotten not made. We try to put into finite phrase what is beyond finite comprehension. Christ, Son of God, is not subordinate to the Father. The Mystery of the Trinity. Father and Son, but one God. That is the nearest we can, and dare, go. In order to make it livable for us, God, in his love, in the Person of the Son, became Man. His Mother was a real woman, but he had no human father: the Holy Spirit, the Third Person of the Trinity, descended upon her. Hence her Child – perfect Man and perfect God:

Who for our sakes and for our salvation came down from heaven and was incarnate of the Holy Spirit and the Virgin Mary and was made Man.

Where are we now in our manifesto of faith? The revelation of the incomprehensible Trinity, three Persons, one God, and the second Person incarnate so that we might dare to see and hear God, not in vision, not as a voice, not in the form of an angel, but in reality.

And was crucified also for us under Pontius Pilate, and he suffered and was buried.

Now the Creed gives no explanation as to why He needed to be crucified, to suffer and to be buried. It simply gives the statement, and the statement of the self-willed death, and of the consequence.

And the third day He rose again, according to the Scriptures. And ascended into heaven, and sitteth on the right hand of the Father.

This is simply the assertion of the truth of the events, without interpretation, precisely a repetition of what we read in the Gospels. This is our 'I believe': our faith in the plain truth of the Gospels. The Creed is essentially simple and simplicity is so often the hardest for our labouring minds to grasp. Just Gospel facts.

And He shall come again with glory to judge the living and the dead, whose Kingdom shall have no end.

And now the promise for the future. The past: He became incarnate, He was crucified, He ascended into heaven. The present: He is in heaven together with the Father. The future: the Day of Judgement. Beyond this we cannot and we need not go.

And in the Holy Spirit, the Lord, the giver of life, who proceedeth from the Father, who with the Father and the Son together is worshipped and glorified, who spake by the prophets.

So to the Third Person, the Spirit, He who breathes life into creation, breathes courage into our bones, breathes and re-breathes the eternal Truth into our minds as He did into the prophets' minds.

But, there is yet more to the Foundation of our Faith: God: Father, Son, and Holy Spirit. The centuries roll on; how am I to hold on to the pure faith with the assault of discordant voices, the assault of human rationalism, all around? How can I not forget, not misunderstand, not mutilate the Truth according to the fashion of the day? Yes, there is one way, the only safe one to rebuff individual satisfaction, one way of self-immolation, one way of overcoming intellectual pride, one way of denying shifting sands of private generosity:

In one, holy, Catholic, and Apostolic Church.

Fall out of the Church, and personal taste tosses you on the waves of indecision, of the drowning grip of immanent good. Hold fast to the Church and triumphantly, sinful as we are, we dare to conclude the Creed:

I acknowledge one baptism for the remission of sins. I look for the resurrection of the dead. And the life of the ages to come. Amen.

Here is the promise, the fulfilment of the Creed: life beyond life.

THE JESUS PRAYER

Lord, Jesus Christ, Son of God, have mercy upon me, a sinner

The Lord's Prayer is the prayer of the whole Church. The Creed is the affirmation of faith, within the Church, of each single person. The Jesus Prayer: I – myself – in the Church but alone; inside the Communion of Saints but struggling by myself; the cry of my heart. As if forsaken, but the Hand held out to save me from drowning. The Prayer of the Heart. Unceasing Prayer. Endless desolation and eternal comfort. Abandoned but not lost. Vile but pure. Slave and sovereign. The paradox of faith in ceaseless repetition. Monotony beyond excitement. Fracture into unity. The one, glorious unity:

Lord, Jesus Christ, Son of God, have mercy upon me, a sinner.

VII

Three Prophets

SOME THOUGHTS ON OBEDIENCE

I sometimes think that obedience is the most difficult of all the virtues even to begin to achieve. From babyhood onwards, calls to obedience are made on us, too often with no other explanation than 'because I say so!' Thus we grow up with a feeling that obedience is some manner of unjust restriction, limiting, and, at its worst, arbitrary tyranny. School follows early childhood and still the question of obedience pursues us: perhaps it is not surprising that emancipated woman prefers not to promise to obey her husband!

But is obedience such a negative submission as at first it may appear to us? Can it possibly be a means rather than an end in itself? Nothing seems to me as remarkable in the sphere of obedience as the lives of the prophets. These men, throughout the ages, again and again were isolated, scorned, persecuted, for their obedience to the divine will: and, the terror was that, unlike the Commandments, there was nothing to show the world except what they alone heard. They obeyed and, as a result, seemed to those around them to be mad, or indulging their own whims, or concerned with some sort of political or religious threat. Their obedience was to an unseen God, unheard by all but themselves. Sometimes even their courage and faith failed them, for He was indeed unseen and His commands were not easy to fulfil. It is difficult enough to obey the command of a visible master, but to obey Him whom you do not see, and to be left in doubt as to the very truth of your vision, must be nearly beyond human endurance. And this is precisely what the prophets endured: isolation, ridicule, persecution, but, worst of all, no certainty in themselves, other than at rare moments of bliss. Blind obedience.

It is one of the most heartening spiritual adventures to follow the prophets in some of their struggles not to obey what seemed nonsense even to them, and to watch the issue of the conflict. It is even more deeply a matter of wonder to see the working of obedience without question. So we come to three examples of prophetic obedience: the lives of Jonah, Elijah, and St John, Baptist and Forerunner.

THE PROPHET JONAH

Jonah was very angry indeed. There was Nineveh, a great city, full to the brim with every possible evil and wickedness, obviously destined for divine chastisement. And what does God do? Tells him, tells his own faithful and true servant, Jonah, to go to Nineveh and warn it of God's wrath! To warn that iniquitous city and bid it repent before it was too late!

Could Jonah obey such a command? A command, as it seemed to him, to get the better of God by a last-minute repentance and reprieve. He could not obey. The alternative was to flee from the presence of the Lord: and promptly he rose to flee to Tarshish, boarding a ship sailing from Joppa.

To flee from the presence of the Lord! To flee in disobedience! To flee if you are his chosen prophet! And so 'the Lord hurled a great wind upon the sea'. There was a terrible storm, and those aboard suspected that someone guilty was among them. Why else should such calamity befall them? So they cast lots, and inevitably the lot fell on Jonah. The fear was great, fear of the roaring sea, the lashing wind, fear of Jonah in his guilt, fear of Jonah's God who was pursuing them. What was to be done? Wilder and wilder grew the sea, the anger of the Lord was upon them, He must be appeased, the guilty must suffer for the innocent, and Jonah was sacrificed: cast as a peace-offering into the sea.

Jonah had disobeyed God, not out of lack of love, but from the wrong sort of love. He wished to constrict God to his own ideas of right and wrong. God now showed him the mercy which Jonah had denied to Nineveh. He would not let Jonah drown but 'appointed a great fish to swallow up Jonah; and Jonah was in the belly of the fish three days and three nights'. Inside the whale, Jonah sang a hymn of praise and love to the Lord, obediently he accepted what the Lord had sent him, but still he did not recognize where his fault lay. And, then, at last, he had his first glimpse of obedience, though he was still far from a full comprehension of the extent of the obedience demanded.

When Jonah was once again safely on dry land, the word of the Lord came to him for the second time, and this time he obeyed and went to Nineveh. Nineveh repented. From the king and his nobles down to the very cattle, there was fasting and sackcloth. Then, God forgave Nineveh and the dreadful punishment of Nineveh was averted.

Jonah's belated obedience saved Nineveh, but still he was blind to the truth and extremely angry. He could not see why Nineveh should be forgiven, and for this very reason he had disobeyed. Now that he had obeyed, the evil city was getting away with it! Jonah went out of the city and settled down to see what happened next. God, in His compassion, gave him the shade of a plant against the heat of the sun, but then a worm came and ate the plant. Jonah then nearly died from the heat and yearned for the plant, and the Lord rebuked him. A mere plant! What about the thousands of human beings who would have perished in Nineveh!

The story of Jonah's disobedience is indeed a consolation and a warning. Again and again we are told in the Gospels not to judge, we are told to forgive, we are told not to be angry one with another. Yet again and again we think we know better – not to judge might be a betrayal of Christianity; to forgive might be weakness or indifference; anger might well be righteous wrath. So we sit and sulk outside our Nineveh. But God, in His mercy, lets us see how even a prophet could have difficulties, and this surely heartens us along our way.

THE PROPHET ELIJAH

Elijah's difficulties with obedience are of another kind from Jonah's. Elijah's difficulties arise from the feeling, only too well-known to us, that he just cannot face any more. Surely no more can be demanded of him! And, every time, something more is demanded! The demands come at every level and at every stage of his active life, and the final call to obedience comes in the burden laid upon him by his disciple, Elisha.

The elder-disciple relationship is only too frequently misinterpreted. The deepest obedience is in the elder, not in the disciple. The disciple does obey his elder, but the elder first must obey the call to self-sacrifice in accepting the burden of a disciple. And his price is by far the heavier.

Before Elisha came to Elijah, we have the moments of despair when obedience seems an imposition beyond human endurance. At Jezebel's threat against his life, Elijah had fled. Exhausted, he longed for death, and he prayed that he might be at last released from an alien, ever hostile, ever lonely world. And the divine command was unrelenting. The angel of the Lord came to Elijah and insisted that he should get up and eat, though all he longed to do was to lie still and die. Yet

Elijah obeyed and he walked forty days and forty nights, retracing the way he had covered with so much pain. God told him to return so that he could anoint Hazael as King of Aram and Jehu as King of Israel. Furthermore, he was to anoint Elisha as his own successor. At this moment, when Elijah had been convinced that his life was ended, that he had nothing more to offer, he was told by God to take to himself a stranger, take him into his innermost heart, and bestow upon him the holy succession of his prophetic spirit.

Elijah did not question. In the total weariness of body and spirit, he obeyed. He saw Elisha ploughing, and, as he passed by, he threw his cloak over him. And Elisha, a man of property, gave up all, and obeyed the call. Obedience passed over into Elisha from Elijah. Elder and disciple. To Elisha alone was granted the joy and the agony of following Elijah in the last days, watching, listening, growing gradually into his suffering: surely in some way a preview of the Apostles' obedience to their Lord.

Elisha's obedience to Elijah is that of disciple to elder. This is not the obedience of prophet to God but it is the initial stage: the silent years of obedience and preparation for the future. The fact that the story is not told as to the manner in which Elijah taught Elisha, or, indeed, the precise matter of the teaching, perhaps throws some light on the mystery of instruction between elder and disciple – the mystery in which obedience plays a major part.

There is in store for the disciple a moment of obedience far more to be dreaded than any other. This is the answer to the call at that moment when he must, in his turn, lead rather than follow. Such an instant of handing over comes with a great force in the last hours of Elijah on earth. In those last hours Elijah and Elisha were left alone. They set out upon their last journey, and Elisha knew, though no word had been spoken, that they were going to Elijah's death. Elisha did not question either the death or the consequences for himself. Elijah offered no comfort to Elisha; he did not even encourage him to remain as his companion. In silence they walked on through the desolate country, the silence only broken by intrusion of the prophets on their way, who told Elisha what he knew only too well. On they went, and again Elijah tried to spare Elisha: 'Stay here'. But love transcends such an order: 'I will not leave you'. And still the voices from outside whisper their warning and Elisha's stern command, 'Be quiet'. Together they go on, 'As the Lord lives and as you yourself live, I will not leave you!' This is obedience to love, refusing the dictates of commonsense, overcoming self-defence.

Together the prophet Elijah and his disciple Elisha crossed the Jordan. Elijah asked Elisha for his last request. How could obedience go further? The elder asks his disciple, and his disciple's yearning desire – the gift to suffer twice as much as his master, the gift to inherit twice his poverty. And, in obedience to God, true to his whole life,

Elijah could not give of his own will: God alone could grant or refuse the request.

The horses of fire bore Elijah away, and Elisha was left. He picked up the mantle of Elijah to begin again the long road of obedience.

ST JOHN THE BAPTIST

The prophet Jonah struggled with his obedience to God, the prophet Elijah obeyed beyond his strength and imperceptibly taught the prophet Elisha to obey, but what of St John the Baptist, the Forerunner? His was, indeed, a life of obedience from the day of his birth.

The birth and childhood of St John the Baptist

We are so used to hearing the story of the birth of our Lord and Saviour Jesus Christ that I am sure we may often forget the significance of the first words in the familiar account of the Annunciation: 'And in the sixth month the angel Gabriel was sent from God . . .' (Luke 1:26). What sixth month? The sixth month of Mary's cousin Elizabeth's pregnancy, who 'well stricken in years' was chosen to give birth to the Forerunner, Forerunner in time as well as proclamation. And the first act of obedience on the baby's behalf was on the day of his circumcision: 'and they called him Zacharias after the name of his father. But his mother knew better and 'answered and said, "Not so; but he shall be called John"' (Luke 1:60).

Elizabeth's obedience to a divine decree is maintained by her husband. who, unable to speak, 'wrote, saying, His name is John . . . And his mouth was opened immediately'. (Luke 1:63-4). So the child was named in obedience, and the obedience dedicated him to the service of God, and to the Son who was to be born six months later. We hear no more of his childhood other than that he 'grew, and waxed strong in spirit'. A dedicated child, as many a prophet before him, but one favoured above all others, for he was to see Him whom they foretold; he was to see and touch the Unseeable, the Untouchable. John was destined to justify all the blind obedience of the prophets who had seen in their minds, in their hearts. What they had foreseen in the dark, he would see in radiant light. But he must prepare.

The wilderness

We remember how Christ himself obeyed the challenge of the Devil. Christ listened to the temptations, so blatantly enticing and worldly. He showed their empty worldliness, but this He could not have done if He had refused to listen. We may pray 'lead us not into temptation', but He, and the greatest of His prophets, and the Saints in their turn, have freely met and overcome these temptations in order that in our turn we might be strengthened and directed by their strength.

Thus, in obedience to the demand God makes on those whom He loves, John prepared for his ministry in the wilderness. There, for a long time, he survived, with the roughest of clothing, the scantiest of food: 'his raiment of camel's hair, and a learthern girdle about his loins; and his meat was locusts and wild honey' (Matthew 3:4). But, as Saints were to discover throughout all the following centuries, life in the wilderness is only ever a preparation. As St Seraphim was to open his cell door many years later, so St John left his solitude to call the erring sheep of Israel to repentance in time to meet the Shepherd. St John was the Forerunner: conceived before his Lord, born before his Lord, and, now, in his manhood, heralding his Lord to His ministry and sacrifice.

The work of St John the Baptist

St John's work in the world began with the cry to repentance – unlike the prophet Jonah, he left his solitude in answer to the divine command in order to prepare the people. His work, like Jonah's, was to turn the people to repentance that they might not be blind to Him who would follow: 'And he came into all the country about Jordan, preaching the baptism of repentance for the remission of sins'. His whole aim was this work of preparation for Him who would follow: 'Prepare ye the way of the Lord, make his paths straight' (Luke 3:4). Of himself there was no thought: only obedience to the divine call.

It was during this time of open ministry that John not only called men to repentance, but that he taught them how to pray, much more explicitly, it would seem, than Christ himself. He fasted and directed his disciples to fast according to the Law. Preaching repentance, he cleansed the people who repented, by baptism in the waters of the Jordan, and this was to be one great test of his obedience.

The baptism of our Lord and Saviour Jesus Christ

How could John obey and baptize his Lord and Master? 'Then cometh Jesus from Galilee to Jordan unto John to be baptized of him' (Matthew 3:13). His first reaction is one of horrified refusal: 'I have need to be baptized of thee, and comest thou to me?' Yet he must do it. If he would not baptize our Lord then the precise unfolding of our salvation would be marred, for more than one aspect of salvation was revealed at the Baptism.

Stepping into the water, Jesus Christ in His Divinity, blessed the waters of the Jordan, and thereby blessed the act of baptism through immersion in water for all time. He gave us, with His own holy body, the essential passport of baptism for salvation. By His own presence, the waters were made holy, and by the hands of his Apostles, and of those ordained by them, the waters for baptism would be made holy from generation to generation. Christian baptism was blessed by God Himself. Christ, perfect God and perfect Man; as God, Christ blessed the waters, but in submitting to baptism at the hands of a man, He asserted the fullness of the truth of His Incarnation. Without sin, yet for our sakes, He suffered baptism that we might learn from Him and be baptized in the waters which He blessed and by which He was blessed. As God and Man, he was acknowledged by His Father in heaven: 'This is my beloved Son, in whom 1 am well pleased'. Grace came upon Him, through baptism; the promise for us: 'the Spirit of God descending like a dove, and lighting upon him' (Matthew 3:16-17). Without John's humble obedience, all this could not have happened.

The humility of St John the Baptist

This humility persisted. The people flocked to John, and he had his disciples. However, his one desire was to hand over to the true Saviour, to redirect people and disciples to Him whom he only heralded: 'I am not the Christ, but that 1 am sent before Him'. Here follow perhaps the most beautiful words of undemanding love to be found in the Gospels, the words of a true prophet who only sees himself as the voice of God, who makes no claim for himself in his own right. How Jeremiah would have rejoiced to hear John, how Isaiah would have been glad to pronouce:

> He that hath the bride is the bridegroom: but the friend of the bridegroom, which standeth and heareth him, rejoiceth greatly because of the bridegroom's voice: this my joy therefore is fulfilled. He must increase, but 1 must decrease (John 3:29-30).

The martyrdom of St John the Baptist

St John the Baptist's martyrdom was on one level as silly as many martyrdoms; because of the glory that was his, even sillier. A sensual woman, a drunken husband, a sensual dance, a wild oath, and then cold reality – the beheading of a man beloved of the people, so beloved that the chief priests and elders did not know how to answer Christ in the Temple: 'we fear the people: for all hold John as a prophet' (Matthew 21: 26). Is it the paradoxical Mystery that John, who acknowledged himself only as the Forerunner of Christ, was revered by the people, but Christ Himself, heard the vile cry 'Crucify Him'.

John, the Forerunner – how meticulously, in total obedience to his particular call, he never overstepped the mark of his work. He preceded, he called to repentance, he baptized, but 'John did no miracle: but all things that John spake of this man were true' (John 10:41).

What greater honour can be given to this Saint and Martyr than the recognition of his Master:

He was a burning and a shining light (John 5:35).

VIII

Light

I have been thinking about light in a variety of connotations and, of course, it becomes more and more evident that it is not possible to think of light other than in relation to darkness: we only know light as light because darkness intervenes. If there were no darkness then there would be no measure of contrast and light would not be light as we understand it. So it might be of some interest to look at various kinds of light vis-à-vis various compatible kinds of darkness.

CHAOS – CREATION

Created beings as we are, it is of course beyond our created minds to realize chaos. We can only see pre-creation in created images. But even such images can be terrifying:

> The secrets of the hoary Deep – a dark
> Illimitable ocean, without bound,
> Without dimension; where length, breadth and hight,
> And time, and place, are lost; where eldest Night
> And Chaos, ancestors of Nature, hold

Eternal anarchy, amidst the noise
Of endless wars, and by confusion stand.

Milton: Paradise Lost, Book 2, lines 891-97

It is the darkness of Chaos which is so terrifying: the inexplicable confusion, the shapeless mass, the absence of clarity of form or outline. This darkness of Chaos took shape, took light, became individual component parts of the Universe under the hand of the Almighty. So we are told in Genesis: 'And God said, Let there be light: and there was light.'

I can hardly imagine any words more deeply thrilling than these. And so essentially simple. No, no words of ours can be adequate for something so vast. Darkness, chaos – no shape, no form, no sense. Then the simplicity of sovereignty summed up in four little words: 'Let there be light'. All that is left is for us to worship in silence. 'And there was light.'

The beginning of the world as we know it, and as we foster it, as we abuse it. Light – without light we could not live; without light, nothing would grow; without light, our hands would be idle.

It is worth remembering that 'God divided the light from the darkness', not only as division of day and night – God divided the light from the darkness. All is within his Providence; all has a meaning. If He gives light, so too He gives darkness.

DIVINE LIGHT

After Jacob wrestled with God, 'as he passed over Penuel the sun rose upon him' (Genesis 32:31). God created light, and ever since man has associated light with God. Light – radiance, illumination reveals all; nothing, under the blaze of light, can be hid. And, as God alone is without sin, He is Light. A blazing, searing Light before which we can only fall down in trembling awe. God alone has power over created light; He alone can make it shine or not: 'with clouds he covereth the light; and commandeth it not to shine . . .' (Job 36:32). God is light. 'The Lord is my light and my gladness' (Psalm 26 [27]). And there is the prophetic promise of Light beyond light:

> The sun shall be no more thy light by day; neither for brightness shall the moon give light unto thee . . . for the Lord shall be thine everlasting light, and the days of thy mourning shall be ended (Isaiah 60: 19–20).

Surely, however, the most exciting, the deepest thrill of anticipation, the greatest call to active service, is the Divine Light in Person, Son of God:

A light to lighten the Gentiles, and the glory of thy people Israel (Luke 2:32).

Christ, our Saviour, His birth gloriously announced in light to the shepherds: 'and the glory of the Lord shone round about them'. Christ, the light that no darkness could contain: 'and the light shineth in darkness; and the darkness comprehended it not.' Christ, Son of God, in His tender love, granted His beloved Apostles the vision of His divinity, the vision that should give them the strength to teach, to witness the Resurrection, and to be martyred:

And after six days Jesus taketh Peter, James, and John his brother, and bringeth them up into the high mountain apart, and was transfigured before them: and his face did shine as the sun, and his raiment was white as the light (Matthew 17:1-2).

Light – again and again – light: symbol of divinity, purity, truth, Transfiguration – seeing the true reality. It was light that met the persecuting Saul on the road to Damascus: 'and suddenly there shined round about him a light from heaven' (Acts 9:3). And it was light that irradiated the first martyr Stephen, who saw the glory of God, and 'fell asleep' (Acts 7:60).

ANGELS AND DEVILS

Light and darkness manifest the constant juxtaposition of good and evil: on the one hand there is light, dazzlng with its beauty, translucent and glorious; on the other hand darkness, repulsive in its very obscurity. From the light stream rays that fill us with awe, yet warm and encourage us at the same moment. But out of darkness comes only dread. The one creative, the other static; the one positive, the other negative. Light is life and darkness is death. For the darkness of evil is not the comforting, healing darkness of night, the repose of sleep, the time of growth. The darkness of evil is not the counterpart of light but its antithesis. Day (light), night (darkness) are one, as sun and moon are one. But light of good and darkness of evil are opposites. The tragedy is that once they also were as one. Is not Satan a fallen angel?

Angels

Angels are messengers of God. Sometimes, particularly for the ancient Jews, they were in fact manifestations of God Himself. Who were the three men whom Abraham entertained? (Genesis 18:2ff). Allegorically, these three men have been seen as the Trinity. Certainly, they were angels. And Jacob's dream (Genesis 28:12)

– a ladder between earth and heaven and 'the angels of God ascending and descending upon it'. It was an angel who came to Elijah, as he lay in despair, and strengthened him, told him to rise and eat. It was an angel who came to Manoah and his barren wife. After his visitation the woman bore Samson, but for Manoah, when 'the angel of the Lord ascended in the flame of the altar', it seemed as if he had witnessed a divine visitation: 'we shall surely die because we have seen God'. So Samson, ironically enough, was conceived in light. But, it was the ass, not Balaam, who saw the angel of the Lord barring the way, for his eyes, in his disobedience, were closed to the light. Angels of light. Bright messengers of God. Warriors of God. Could not Christ have summoned more than twelve legions of angels, had he so wished, against the powers of darkness (Matthew 26:53)? And when Christ, perfect God and perfect Man, fasted and was tempted in the desert, did not angels come to minister unto him? From the darkness of temptation to the light of healing.

Birth and Resurrection. It was the Angel Gabriel who heralded the Light of the World. And where the body had lain, two angels sat, the one at the head, the other at the feet.

Devils

Sin inevitably is relative: it has no autonomous life but depends as a parasite on a welcoming host. Devils, fallen angels of light, are dark: they have no existence other than as corrupt light. Devils lurk inside the heart of man, the mind of man, the very soul of man. They find comfortable nests in the darkness within us. But, when they are expelled, even then they seek further shelter from the radiant truth of light, and entering the swine hurtle into the waves below.

Devils, angels of night, can only work furtively, secretly, discerning our weakest points of pride, ambition, envy, and nestling into them. One sharp shaft of true light, and they flee – devils are the greatest cowards, and bullies! Darkness is ever their field of activity, for in the darkness of ignorance, or of fear, or of godlessness, they can take shapes never to be achieved in the Light of Truth.

Satan, in all his assumed majesty, knows no approach but temptation. Even Satan, prince of devils, depends on what is, relies on matter, on the tangible: of creative power he knows nothing. His pride is immeasurable, as is his stupidity. How could the Devil dare to tempt his Master and his God? And, yet, he did dare to tempt Him in the wilderness. Did He allow this temptation so that we need not fear? God Himself was tempted. In the temptation, therefore, there is no sin; only in the yielding is there sin. Yes, God showed us how to deal with the Devil, how to answer the temporal with the eternal: 'Man shall not live by bread alone' (Matthew 4:4). How the Devil loathes to leave his comfortable darkness! He implores to be left in peace inside his prey: 'Let us alone; what have we to do with Thee, Thou Jesus of Nazareth? Art Thou come to destroy us?' (Luke 4:34).

What can be more vivid, image though it may be, than the harrowing of hell? The darkness of hell? Prisoners chained to eternal night? And the blazing light of Paschal Saturday: the terror of the devils, trying to bar the doors, to do all in their power to keep out the Light: the Salvation of the world dead and alive. The sun hid its rays at the Crucifixion, but the Light will not be hid.

SIN AND RIGHTEOUSNESS

It is interesting how often sin and righteousness in juxtaposition are seen as some form of darkness and light. Inevitably it is the darkness of ignorance and the light of revelation.

In Isaiah 8:20, we read 'If they speak not according to this word, it is because there is no light in them'. There are numerous examples, both in the Old Testament and in the Gospels, both of the darkness of sin and of the light of righteousness. Sin is often identified with ignorance and righteousness with enlightenment. But, for me, some examples from the Gospel of St John are particularly evocative where the darkness of sin is concerned.

Nicodemus

Nicodemus was afraid, afraid for his position as a ruler of the Jews, afraid for his social status, afraid, as so many are today, of losing his job by backing the wrong side. Yet he felt himself drawn to the new, strange Teacher: he could not keep away. But what about loss of prestige? Hence, he 'came to Jesus by night'. He came furtively, as if it were a deed of evil, and, paradoxically, coming in darkness, he found light:

Light is come into the world, and men loved darkness rather than light, because their deeds were evil. For every one that doeth evil hateth the light, neither cometh to the light, lest his deeds should be reproved (John 3:19-20).

St John the Baptist

St John the Baptist, Forerunner, Herald of Christ God – how beautifully Christ describes him as 'a burning and a shining light', flame of truth, the searing fire of holiness, fire that cleanses and destroys, light that shows the way to Truth, and light that sees into the innermost being of sin. And, if St John the Baptist is the heralding light, then how forcefully come the words of the actual Light, the living Presence. Lights – holy lights – there have been, and lights – holy lights – there will be, but there IS only the One:

I am the light of the world: he that followeth me shall not walk in darkness, but shall have the light of life (John 8:12).

What a promise! Christ, the light into the world. And the light is not static; it is a working light that we, as Christians, must shine into the world of darkness to the utmost of our meagre individual capacity.

The light of Christ's righteousness transfers upon the work of the Apostles:

Ye are the light of the world . . . let your light so shine before men, that they may see your good works, and glorify your Father which is in heaven (Matthew 5:16).

The light of righteousness: the Christian demand upon each of us according to our capacity. At baptism we receive enlightenment and from then on we must 'walk as children of light' (Ephesians 5:8). We must take upon us the whole armour of God – the brilliant armour reinforced not by metal links but by the light of the living Christ.

BLINDNESS AND SIGHT

Many of us at some time in our lives have wondered what could be the worst ill that could befall us. Which of our faculties would be the most dreadful to lose? I think (I do not know about others) that my particular horror has always been the thought of blindness. If I could not hear, I could still read; if I could not walk, I could still listen to music; if I could not speak, I could still walk in the fields. Blindness has been, for me, the nightmare thought. So, perhaps, I have been particularly alive to the wretchedness of the blind people in the Gospels, and the unbelievable gladness of the miracles of sight.

Blindness of body, and blindness of spirit:

And thou shalt grope at noon-day, as the blind gropeth in darkness . . . (Deuteronomy 28:29).

I was eyes to the blind, and feet was I to the lame (Job 29:15).

The promise:

And in that day . . . the eyes of the blind shall see out of obscurity . . . (Isaiah 29:18).

And the fulfilment, the actual miracles of healing:

> And their eyes were opened (Matthew 9:30).
> And unto many that were blind he gave sight (Luke 7:21).
> He put clay upon mine eyes, and I washed, and do see (John 9:15).

The significance of spiritual blindness vis-à-vis the physical:

> If ye were blind, ye should have no sin: but now ye say, We see; therefore
> your sin remaineth (John 9:41).

This is the sin – the dreadful sin of sins – the sin of double ignorance: the sin of thinking we know what we do not know. This is the sin, the deepest sin against the Holy Spirit, the sin of pitting the finite intellect against Divine Wisdom; the presumption that we can achieve the knowledge of what is outside our human capacity.

Is there anything more exciting than the joy of the blind man as normal sight returned to him? At first he saw 'men as trees, walking', all out of focus, but then came the revelation: 'he was restored and saw every man clearly' (Mark 8:24-5). How often are we granted to see every man clearly? Or the two blind men who faithfully dogged Christ's footsteps until in pity he touched 'their eyes, saying, According to your faith be it unto you'. According, in the measure, of their faith. Unrelenting pursuit of faith. Call, and call again.

Blindness and the terror of it. The horror of sentimental comment. I find Siegfried Sassoon's 'Does it Matter?' one of the most heart-rending comments on blindness: the soldier, blinded in war, and the silly people with their superficial, silly comments of comfort – comfort for the blind or their own uneasy conscience?

> There's such splendid work for the blind.

One of the most cynically dreary lines of English war poetry:

> And people will always be kind,
> As you sit on the terrace remembering
> And turning your face to the light.

The devastating torment of kindness. Better perhaps the agony of Samson, blind in the blaze of noon, but with revenge in his power. He was not helpless. But, better still, the momentary forgetting of self, that rare capacity for going beyond personal agony into some glimpse of the Divine Will. How many of us could even think of that exquisite line of faith:

They also serve who only stand and wait (Milton, *On his blindness*).

THE APOCALYPSE

The revelation granted to the beloved Apostle gives us this final image of light: the ultimate promise. The whole book of the Apocalypse is redolent of the balanced contrasts of darkness and light, and finally of the last battle between the darkness of evil and the light of good. And it contains the greatest revelation of all, the greatest promise for the new life – light will no longer be the antithesis of darkness, relativity will cease.

And there shall be no night there; and they need no candle, neither light of the sun; for the Lord giveth them light (Apocalypse 22:5).

In this promise of what will be, we light our candles at Easter. The Light, Christ, is risen, and there is no more the darkness of the grave. Joy replaces sorrow. Our flickering faith joins in the great, swelling sea of the grace of prayer.

This seems, indeed, the moment to listen to John Tavener's searing *Ikon of Light* and his *New Jerusalem* of the *Apocalypse*.

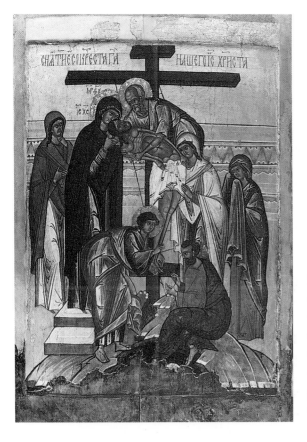

IX

Holy Week

In this chapter, 1 should like to be much more factual than 1 have been up to now. 1 should like to take you with me on the journey of Holy Week, tell you a little of what each day means to us and how we keep it, and so take you to the climax, the peak of the Christian life: the Resurrection.

Holy Week, in its individuality, stands out completely from the rest of the year. We wait for it and dread that something may happen to mar the peace and isolation: it is the one week in the year when we have always shut our doors and allowed ourselves blessed silence from the outside world, as it were to stoke up our fires of charity.

Holy Week is only one week, but ever and again a lifetime, and a life-line. Our whole concentration lies in the services, services lived through in the whole Orthodox world from generation to generation, services that have their particular 'highlights' known and awaited by the people.

HOLY MONDAY TO HOLY WEDNESDAY

Holy Monday begins with Vespers on Palm Sunday evening, for the Orthodox liturgical cycle begins at the setting of the sun on the previous day. And the six verses sung alternately with the final six verses of the opening psalms still speak of the glory of the entry into Jerusalem, but also foretell the betrayal to follow:

The saddle on the foal foretells in image the tumult of the nations turning over from unfaith to faith . . .

With the verses of the *Aposticha* (verses sung at the end of Vespers and at the end of Matins) comes the command:

Away from palms and branches, as passing on to a divine feast, let us the faithful hasten together to the worship of the Passion of Christ, the mystery of Salvation . . .

And the first of many reproaches, as true to us today, Christian in name, as they were to the rulers of the Jews:

Why do you boast in the Father, rejecting the Son? May you then be shamed by your own children, thus crying out: Hosanna to the Son of David, blessed is he who comes in the name of the Lord.

Vespers and Compline still have as part of their ending the prayer that has accompanied us throughout the Great Lent, other than on Sundays, which is the day of Resurrection whatever the season. It is the prayer of St Ephrem, the prayer of contrition and repentance. It is said in church and at home:

O Lord and Master of my life, give me not a slothful spirit, meddlesome, lustful of power, and vain of word. (*Full prostration*)

But a spirit sober, humble, patient and loving, grant to me, your servant. (*Full prostration*)

Yea, O Lord King, grant me to see my own transgressions, and not to judge my brother, for you are blessed unto the ages of ages. Amen. (*Full prostration*)

O God, cleanse me a sinner. (*Said twelve times with twelve bows to the ground*)

O Lord and Master of my life . . . (*all the way through without stopping and ending with a full prostration*)

But it is with Monday Matins that we seem to be entering fully into Holy Week. Matins during Holy Week is normally celebrated late on the previous evening; the exact time varies according to local custom. Thus, we begin our Monday of Holy Week on Sunday night. Although all is said or sung as usual, for many Orthodox the long-expected moment comes with the singing of the *Troparion* (a short hymn) sung only at Matins on Monday, Tuesday, and Wednesday of Holy Week. Some people even refer to the whole of Matins of these three days as the Service of the Bridegroom: whatever the melody of the national Orthodox tradition, whatever the language, for all of us, traditionally, this herald of Holy Week is very precious:

> Behold the Bridegroom comes in the middle of the night: and blessed is the servant whom he finds watching: but unworthy he whom he finds heedless. See to it, then, my soul, not to be weighed down by sleep, lest you be handed over to death and shut out from the Kingdom: but rouse yourself crying: Holy, Holy, Holy is God: through the prayers of the Mother of God, have mercy upon us.

This hymn introduces for us all the pain and joy of Holy Week. And this hymn is later followed in Matins of Monday to Thursday with the equally loved one of the *Exapostilarion* following the recital of the Odes of the Canon:

> Your bridal chamber I see adorned, O my Saviour, and I have not the garment that I may enter in: O give light to the raiment of my soul, Giver of Light, and save me.

These two hymns mark out Matins of the first part of Holy Week from any other Matins of the year, but of course all the verses of every prayer and hymn are relevant to the journey on which we have embarked. I cannot possibly do more within the compass of this chapter than give a few hints of the wealth of repentance to which we are called:

> Judas lusts after money in his mind . . . O Christ God, deliver us from his lot
> . . .

> Lover of man, Christ God, grant forgiveness of sins to those who worship in faith your pure Passion.

> . . . Come then, let us also, with minds purified, go with Him, and be crucified with Him, and die for Him to the delights of life . . .

. . . Brethren, fearful of the punishment of the withered fig tree because it bore no fruit, let us bring fruits worthy of repentance to Christ, granting us great mercy.

. . . The Harlot came up to you and poured myrrh with tears on your feet, O Lover of mankind, and by your command she is redeemed from the filthy smell of evil deeds . . .

Yes, Monday to Wednesday Matins live for us in the deep, deep plunge into repentance, with our self-identification with all treachery and evil, and, above all, inadequacy in the face of Christ's love. How can we escape from being shut out? And to remind ourselves ever and ever again of the Truth, we face the Gospels as if we have never previously heard them.

During the Hours of Monday, Tuesday and Wednesday, we read all four Gospels from beginning to end, but stopping at Chapter 13, verse 31, of St John. It is a great journey, and a strange one, for however often during the year we have read extracts from the Gospels, now, ever and again, we find something that strikes us as quite new, or in an unexpected place and, when read fully in context, passages can take on strange emphasis, or even a different meaning.

Into these first three days of Holy Week we seem to pack everything which we possibly can: all the Psalms are read, the cycle is completed of the Old Testament readings in the Sixth Hour and Vespers. For those three days we are somehow still in the world, in the realm of events, completing the long journey of the Great Lent. And then – the step is taken into the furnace of fire: the Mystery, Mystery of the Last Supper, the Washing of Feet, the betrayal, the Crucifixion, the stillness of the tomb. It hardly seems possible for so much to be experienced between Holy Thursday and midnight of Holy Saturday, and yet it is experienced year after year. Here, I can only give a glimpse of what can only be experienced in the fullness of the church services.

HOLY THURSDAY

On Thursday we experience the Washing of the Feet, and the betrayal:

Taking the bread into his hands, the betrayer secretly reaches out and clutches the price for Him who fashioned man with His own hand: and he remained incorrigible, Judas, slave and traitor.

Judas betrays, and we, at the Holy Liturgy of St Basil, remember first and foremost the institution of Holy Communion. Again and again we sing the one hymn appointed for Holy Thursday, replacing the customary ones with this awesome self-dedication:

> Of your mysterious supper, Son of God, today admit me a partaker. For I will not speak of the mystery to your enemies, nor give you a kiss as Judas, but as the thief I will confess you. Remember me, Lord, when you come into your kingdom. Alleluia. Alleluia. Alleluia.

At the completion of the Liturgy, there follows the symbolical washing of the feet, normally, in cathedrals and monasteries.

We have now reached the moment of betrayal.

HOLY FRIDAY

Holy Friday is the one day in the year when the Divine Liturgy may not be celebrated. It is a day of total fasting, not only from food and drink, but even from the Gifts of the Holy Body and Blood of our Lord Jesus Christ. It is a day dedicated to our sin, His Crucifixion.

Matins of Holy Friday, normally celebrated on Thursday night, is known as the Matins of the Twelve Gospels: twelve times the Gospel is read, and it takes us step by step through the terror of the betrayal, beginning with St John 13:31 to 18:1 – Christ's disclosing of Himself to His chosen Apostles; the true vine; the promise of the Comforter; the warning of their martyrdoms to come; the promise of the future Coming; the prayer for his chosen ones:

> And all mine are thine, and thine are mine; and I am glorified in them . . .
> that the love wherewith thou hast loved me may be in them, and I in them.

The last Gospel reading is St Matthew 27:66:

> So they went, and made the sepulchre sure, sealing the stone, and setting a watch.

Twelve times, inexorably, we listen to the betrayal and the Crucifixion. The words may vary, but the facts hammer inexorably into our very pulse beats:

> Today Judas . . . senselessly prefers thirty pieces of silver to the love of the Lord.

Today they pierced His side with a sword who scourged Egypt with plagues for their sake and they gave Him gall to drink who rained down manna upon them for food.

And we listen to the heart-rending appeal to Judas, sung by one specially appointed, standing in the middle of the church:

What was there, Judas, in his behaviour to make you betray the Saviour? Did he cut you off from the company of the Apostles? Did he deprive you of the grace of healing? Did he turn you away from the table when you were at supper with the others? When he washed the others' feet did he scorn yours? Oh, how many blessings you have forgotten! But while your ungrateful mind is published abroad in its infamy, his immeasurable long-suffering is proclaimed, and his great mercy.

On Holy Friday, we meet in church at some time between two and four o'clock in the afternoon according to local custom. In prayer we accompany Joseph of Arimathea in his act of faithful and courageous mercy: the body is taken down from the Cross and wrapped in the shroud; and as Vespers comes to its close, the shroud is brought out from the Sanctuary and carried in procession to be laid in the middle of the church. We throw flowers upon it, as tokens of the spices hastily placed on the body before the Sabbath, or perhaps we have already prepared a glorious flower-bedecked shroud. And we sing:

Noble Joseph took your pure body down from the tree, and when he had wrapped it in clean linen with sweet spices, he laid and enclosed it within a new tomb.

The second hymn, sung directly afterwards, already holds the promise:

The angel, standing at the tomb, cried aloud to the women bearing myrrh: myrrh is fitting for the dead, but Christ has shown himself a stranger to corruption.

Vespers sees the taking down from the Cross, but Matins, which follows later that night, continues from the taking down to the placing in the new tomb, and the setting of the watch. Already, even at the moment of mortal death, we hear the promise:

Do not weep for me, Mother, as you see in the tomb the Son whom you conceived in your womb without seed: for I shall rise and be glorified and as God will exalt in glory those who unceasingly magnify you in faith and love.

The procession winds its way to the tomb for the burial, the shroud is placed in the middle of the church.

The hand of the Lord . . . set me down in the midst of the valley; it was full of bones . . . Thus says the Lord God to these bones: Behold, I will cause breath to enter into you . . . and the breath came into them, and they lived . . . And I will put my Spirit within you and you shall live . . . (Ezekiel 37:1, 5, 10, 14).

We venerate the shroud, and many of the faithful remain all night in church, praying and guarding the tomb until the morning dawns.

HOLY SATURDAY

Holy Saturday always seems to me a time somehow suspended out of time. We see the tomb. We hear the first great cry:

Rise, O God, judge the earth, for all the peoples are your dominion.

We have lived through forty days in the wilderness of the Great Lent; we have walked step by step to the Crucifixion in Holy Week. Now, on Holy Saturday, the readings from the Prophets tell us what to expect, as does the Liturgy of the day; and, yet, year after year, I find it almost impossible to believe. Are we once again really, in mind, heart, and soul, to experience the Resurrection? Are we not too weary this year? Will strength and joy once again flood in as they have always done? Will this miracle of experience visit us once more?

EASTER DAY

As midnight approaches, we gather in church; it is dark, cold, and we are sleepy. And – suddenly! Once again we are seized as if by the holy fire of inspiration and from afar we hear the voices singing the first acclamation of the Resurrection. The procession winds its way, candles lit, to the church door:

Your Resurrection, O Christ Saviour, angels are singing in the heavens, and on earth make us worthy with pure hearts to glorify you.

Bells are ringing! Lights! Voices! Censers! And for the first time the glorious words rise to heaven, the words that will be sung again and again at this Paschal Feast, and every day until the Feast of the Ascension:

> Christ is risen from the dead, death He trampled down by death, and to those in the tombs He has given life.

Greek, Slavonic, English – in all the languages of the world, in all melodies, let the whole universe rejoice:

> Christ is risen!
> He is risen indeed!

And, as we enter into the Paschal Feast, year after year, we hear the gracious, welcoming words of St John Chrysostom. We are sinners indeed, we have not laboured throughout the day in the vineyard, but yet we are welcomed. On this glorious Feast of the Resurrection, all are welcomed to the Feast of Feasts – rich and poor, virtuous and sinful. There is no limit to divine hospitality on this, the day of Resurrection:

> If any be devout and a lover of God let him enjoy this beautiful and radiant festival. If any be a grateful servant let him enter rejoicing into the joy of his Lord. If any be weary with fasting let him now receive his penny. If any have laboured from the first hour let him today receive his due payment. If any have come after the third hour let him feast gratefully. And he that arrived only after the sixth hour let him in no wise hesitate for he too shall suffer no loss. And if any have delayed to the ninth hour let him approach also without hesitation. And he that has arrived only at the eleventh hour let him not be afraid of his delay: for the Master is bountiful and receives the last as the first: he gives rest to him who comes at the eleventh hour as well as to him who laboured from the first: and he gives to one, and bestows upon the other, and he accepts the work and approves the endeavour and honours the act and commends the intention. Thus all may enter into the joy of our Lord: the first, and those who come after, receive your reward. Rich and poor, make glad together. Sober and slothful celebrate the day. You who have fasted, and you who have not fasted, rejoice today. The table is full, eat sumptuously, all of you. Let your bodies be nourished, let no one leave hungry. The calf is fat, let no one go hungry away. Let all partake of the cup of faith. Let all partake of the riches of goodness. Let no one mourn at

poverty: for the universal kingdom has been revealed. Let no one lament his transgressions, for forgiveness has risen from the tomb. Let no one fear death, for the death of the Saviour has freed us. He quenched it by enduring it. He destroyed hell when he went down to hell. Hell was embittered when it tasted of his flesh. Isaiah foretold this when he cried out, saying, Hell was embittered when it met you below: it was embittered for it is made void: it was embittered for it is mocked: embittered for it has been slain: embittered for it is overpowered: embittered for it is fettered. It received a body and it discovered God: it took earth and met Heaven: it took what it saw and was overcome by what it did not see. O death, where is your sting? O Hell, where is your victory? Christ is risen, and you are laid low. Christ is risen, and the demons have fallen. Christ is risen and the angels rejoice. Christ is risen, and life is set free. Christ is risen, and none dead in the tomb: for Christ risen from the dead has become the first fruits of those fallen asleep. To him be glory and power, unto the ages of ages.

Amen.

Gospel Thoughts

1. For whosoever will save his life shall lose it (Matthew 16:25).

The modern fashion of parading the body, of finding beauty in immodesty, of nothing causing shame, of the climax of self-admiration, is funda-mentally absurd. Behaviour such as this denies the Fall and advocates a self-made paradise; it denies the necessity of Christ's work of salvation; it denies repentance; it denies humility; it is in fact a suicidal perpetuation of the Fall – unintelligent arrogance.

2. Rejoice with me for I have found my sheep which was lost (Luke 15:6).

I will give unto the last even as unto thee (Matthew 20:14).

Martha, Martha, thou art careful and troubled about many things; but one thing is needful; and Mary hath chosen that good part (Luke 10:41-42).

The work of love is sometimes hidden; it is no longer an actual doing but it is the work of the spectator. His work of love is gladly to rejoice in the spiritual triumph or ascetic work of another; actively not to grudge.

3. Jesus saith unto him, if I will that he tarry till I come, what is that to thee
    . . . ? (John 21:22).

St Peter must not allow his life to be relative. Each of us has specific work to do, and what our neighbour does, whether he be Mr Smith or St John, or how he is repaid, lies not on the road of salvation.

4. Simon, launch out into the deep and let down your nets for a draught . . .
    (Luke 5:4).

Peter doubted this command, he had fished all night and had caught nothing. Yet he obeyed, and was rewarded. Doubt for all of us is unavoidable; but to act faithfully within the doubt is our work.

5. Heaven and earth shall pass away; but my words shall not pass away
    (Mark 13:31).

The Gospel is a Mystery: it is not a book of texts for scholars but an invitation, a demand, a trumpet-call for human faith. The Gospel is always itself, in whatever century, in whatever part of the universe: ever present, never past, never future.

6. Verily, verily, I say unto you, he that entereth not by the door into the
    sheepfold, but climbeth up some other way, the same is a thief and a robber
    (John 10:1).

An explicit divine command for one door: the Holy Apostolic Church, founded on the Rock, guarded and enriched by Tradition, established by God Incarnate. However rationally and humanly acceptable, no fundamental change has been authorized. 'A wise man builds his house upon a rock' (Matthew 7:25); let the winds of fashion blow, but his house will not fall.

7. Then spake Jesus to the multitude, and to his disciples, saying, the Scribes
    and the Pharisees sit in Moses' seat: all therefore whatever they bid you
    observe, that observe and do; but do not ye after their works; for they say,
    and do not (Matthew 23:1-3).

A very comforting passage if ever we are disturbed by the private lives of our priests. We must listen for their words which come from the Gospels, from the Fathers, from their own true minds, but we must not be influenced by their day-to-day behaviour. Their words may well be of the Spirit even if their behaviour is of the world.

8. Then Jesus said to His disciples, If any man will come after Me, let him deny himself, take up his cross, and follow Me (Matthew 16:24).

Why do we always imagine that our cross comes from the outside? From objectionable people, from poverty, from illness? The Cross was of Christ's own will, not imposed upon Him. Surely our crosses are our own: our sins, our fears, our evil thoughts, and, our repentance. The cross for us must surely be not the evil from outside, but our attitude to the evil. The personal cross is to avoid human influence, not to depend on human admiration and praise.

9. . . . There was a dead man carried out, the only son of his mother . . . and he came and touched the bier: and they that bare him stood still. And he said, Young man, I say unto thee, Arise. And he that was dead sat up . . . (Luke 7:12-15).

No miracle is possible without faith, not necessarily the faith of the sick: the young man was dead. But, those who carried him stood still. That was enough. A widow's mite. A grain of mustard seed.

10. And beside all this, between us and you there is a great gulf fixed (Luke 16:26).

Here is the horrifying story of the fate of the rich man when he died. He, who had 'fared sumptuously every day', on dying went into the parching thirst of hell, while Lazarus, the beggar at his gate, reposed in Abraham's bosom. There was no hope for the rich man nor yet for his brothers still alive. No help, apparently, could reach him – this gulf between heaven and hell. But, is it really so for us sinners? Christ rose from the dead. There is no gulf, for Christ stands in the gulf: Christ is the gulf. If we repent, then, with the thief, this night we shall be with Him in Paradise.

11. Watch therefore, for ye know neither the day nor the hour wherein the Son of man cometh (Matthew 25:13).

Does this only apply to the last day, the Day of Judgement? Or can it also mean that we must be ever watchful? We do not know when Christ comes: is He coming now in that tramp? In that child? At work? On holiday? Next door? In church? We never know when Christ comes. Certainty is not for us, but in faith we may take risks.

12. And he saith unto them, whose is this image and superscription? (Matthew 22:20).

Tribute money was improperly demanded of Christ and his Apostles. Sometimes, rather than fighting, it is better to follow an unjust demand to its logical conclusion. Money is of the world: it bears the face of an earthly ruler. Thus, rather than cause trouble, it is better to obey a worldly demand, even if unjust, provided it does not encroach on any spiritual betrayal. The demand was unfair, but there was no blasphemy in it. We need not always stand on our secular rights, but treat them as unimportant – pay out of our daily earnings.

13. Behold, a sower went forth to sow . . . (Matthew 13:3).

In the Parable of the Sower, the sower is remarkable for his prodigality. He scattered seed far and wide: the divine generosity. There is no question of predestination: the seed fell everywhere and the earth was free to receive or reject according to its nature. In His divine providence He knew who would betray Him. Yet He scattered to Judas as well as to Peter and John.

John Tavener and the Music of Paradise – A Commentary

John Tavener's view that music is a means of praising the Creator is, as he has himself observed on various occasions, eccentric (in the true sense of the word) in the late twentieth century; and yet all composers of genuinely sacred music in whatever age have been in accord with him.

Knowledge of the traditions of chanting in religious ritual is essential for a composer who wants to enter creatively into the musical aspect of a religious tradition. Chant falls between the spontaneous musical communication with or celebration of the divine and composed music. Certainly in Christian traditions chant was composed; it did not simply appear. Rather, the composer is of little importance – he is a craftsman in the same way as an ikon painter, a cathedral mason, or a maker of stained-glass windows, whose work becomes part of a greater whole in the service of God. His name may be forgotten.

It is of course unlikely that John Taverner's name will be forgotten, by reason of that very eccentricity which he finds characteristic of his position. He is not a craftsman within what Eric Gill would have called a 'holy tradition of working', but a composer writing sacred music (which may or may not correspond with the writing of liturgical music) in a society wholly secular in its orientation.

Tavener looks back and tries to recover Paradise lost – he has quoted Dostoyevsky's dictum that 'it is only by beauty that the world will be saved'. He does this not by reinventing a spuriously paradisiacal music, but by creating anew a musical vocabulary using as building blocks elements of religious chant, specifically Russian and Byzantine chant. It happens that in much of Tavener's work those chants are audible only to the person who already knows them; often (as, for example, with the melodic material of *The Protecting Veil*) they are used simply as a scaffolding upon which to construct vast melodic lines of great beauty; often too they are dispensed with altogether and their memory (their 'archetypal memory', audible musically) remains and informs his music: it is a language of musical symbolism.

The *Bless* duet from Tavener's 'opera' *Mary of Egypt* has been described as 'Monteverdian', but this is surely to miss the point. The encounter between Mary and Father Zossima in the desert is a sacred dialogue. (As Rudolf Kassner has said, 'In the Kingdom of the Father there is no drama but only dialogue, which is disguised monologue'.) The opera itself is a para-liturgical drama, like the western mediaeval *Visitatio Sepulchri* or *Ludus Danielis*, or the Byzantine drama of the *Three Children in the Furnace*, though these three are more strictly liturgical in that they had an appointed position in the liturgical sequence and arose out of chant.

The element of humanism so fundamental to Monteverdi – as to the entire western 'Renaissance' – is utterly lacking in both Mother Thekla's libretto and in Tavener's music. *Bless* becomes an ecstatic duet (almost a 'vocalize') because it is the only word Mary and Father Zossima have to say to each other. They have gone beyond words. And yet, in saying that one word, begging each other's blessing, they say everything; hence the importance of this moment in the opera. A cascade of ecstatic melody, arising out of the ritualized musical austerity characteristic of the rest of the work, replaces the inability of words to communicate the moment.

I know no other opera quite like *Mary of Egypt*, though precedents may be sought in those mediaeval liturgical dramas. In purely musical terms it may remind the listener of Benjamin Britten's *Church Parables*. Nevertheless, the work attained its shape and its stark musical beauty from necessity – the necessity to present in simple iconic terms the story of Mary of Egypt. This could have been treated in a conventionally operatic way (as indeed it was, by Respighi in his *Maria Equiziaca*), but would hardly have had the elemental spiritual force found in Tavener's music. As with its distant musical relatives, it is not really an opera at all.

The Psalms have traditionally been a rich source of texts for composers of all traditions, the image of David, the singer-king, being particularly attractive to musicians. The Psalms bring with them an entire Jewish musical heritage of which Tavener, in his setting of Psalm 121, *I will lift up mine eyes unto the hills*, was aware, filtered through the Greek Church. As Mother Thekla points out, the Psalms play a very important role in Orthodox liturgical texts.

The piece is marked to be sung 'with Byzantine grandeur', immediately evident musically in the use of the *ison*, or drone. In the ruggedness of the music there is an element of the strength which characterizes so much of the Old Testament, though there is no direct reference to Jewish cantillation, the chanting of the synagogue. The melodic character of the music perhaps emphasizes more the joy and tenderness also to be found in the words; for parallels in the other arts, one might think of the paintings of Marc Chagall or Leonard Cohen's *Book of Mercy*. The universality of the Psalm texts is perhaps indicated by the fact that Tavener's setting was commissioned for and first performed by an Anglican cathedral choir, that of St Paul's in London.

'Little lamb, who made thee? Dost thou know who made thee?' Blake's gnostic and idiosyncratic vision of God encompassed both the innocence of the lamb and, in another poem, the magnificence of the tiger. He had a particular awareness of the ability of the divine to penetrate and interact with the created world.

The lamb is, so to speak, an ikon of the sacrificial lamb who is Christ. The holy potential within the innocent image of the lamb is of course difficult to convey in music. Does Tavener's setting perhaps suggest only the innocence, with its child-like melody sung against itself in inversion and sweetly harmonized? One might say that *The Lamb* finds its fulfilment in *The Tiger*, in which there is a direct musical reference to the former. Yet the lamb reminds us of the finite quality of our created minds and also the infinite splendour and infinite humility inherent in the Incarnation – so perhaps the simplicity and fragility of Tavener's music do justice to the extraordinary nature (both within and outside Nature) of this event. A Blakeian paradox indeed.

With the repentant thief humanity takes a step towards God: one of the crucified thieves asks Christ 'Remember me when Thou comest into Thy Kingdom', and is given the promise 'Today thou shalt be with Me in Paradise'. Tavener's instrumental work *The Repentant Thief* takes as its theme that journey towards Paradise, the thief being seen as a kind of *yurodivy*, an holy fool, blindly dancing towards salvation. Structurally the work is divided up into a series of laments and dances, separated by a recurring refrain. The scoring is for solo clarinet (whose sound has definite overtones for Tavener of the Greek folk instrument, the *clarino*), strings and percussion. The soloist, in the composer's words, 'leads the Dance and the Lament, apparently going nowhere: the human paradox as I perceive it musically, leading to the End Point.' Thus it is that the soloist is not 'arguing' with the ensemble in the manner of a traditional concerto – he is the focal point and at the same time directs the other instruments to their goal (also the case in *The Protecting Veil*). The final dance is transfigured – through its musical stasis we are suddenly aware of the high goal that lies at the end of the apparently aimless dancing, and we enter a realm of timelessness (as we do at the end of Stravinsky's *Symphony of Psalms*, similarly a sacred journey translated into music). As T. S. Eliot put it, 'the fire and the rose shall be one'.

The word *ikon* has been much misused in recent years. Tavener's music – a metaphor, as Mother Thekla says – seeks to enlighten those who have never seen an ikon except as a mere painting or a holy picture. It is a sacred image, a gentle presence, a direct means of communication with the divine but painted (or 'written' in traditional language, but in any case incarnated) with the humble hands of the ikon painter according to traditional patterns and methods.

William Butler Yeats was no Orthodox Christian, but he had a strong intuition for the sacred, as his investigations of Celtic mythology and Indian religion and his membership of the Order of the Golden Dawn show. He also understood the ikon painter's humility in the face of the eternal: though he struggled long and hard to reach his own Byzantium across 'that dolphin-tossed, that gong-tormented sea', he had the simplicity to wish for 'the heavens' embroidered cloths' as both sacred and secular ikon.

Tavener responds to this desire, in one of his rare secular works, scored for soprano, flute, viola and harp, with music of similarly transparent simplicity. There is no strong difference between this spare, chant-like writing and his sacred music. Tavener shows this by using a musical palindrome based on a Byzantine chant played on the harp which separates almost all the songs in the cycle, and which serves to generate the musical material of the songs themselves. Both share the sense of Paradise lost and of the desire to recover it. Here this desire is coupled with the awareness of the loss of the childhood state of innocence, of the 'child dancing in the wind'.

The Mother of God is instrumental in the recovery of Paradise. At the same time a simple maid and the Universal Mother, of cosmic power, she at all times acts as a vessel for the divine: 'Be it unto me according to Thy word.' Tavener's *Annunciation* encapsulates these two aspects of Mary. A quartet of soloists, ideally singing from a gallery, sing the words of the Mother of God – 'How shall this be, seeing I know not a man?' – in response to the main choir, to which is given the words of the Archangel: 'Hail! Thou that art highly favoured. Hail! The Lord is with thee. Hail! Blessed art thou among women.' This builds up, as Tavener says in his preface to the score, to 'a thunderous, awesome theophany'. The contrast between the awesome salutation of Gabriel and the humility and wonder of Mary finds a musical response in the rich chords gradually built up to convey the former, and the brief, gentle phrase, subtly dissonant, given to the latter.

The Orthodox feast of the Protecting Veil commemorates that cosmic power which is also a part of the Mother of God. The feast is kept in remembrance of the appearance of the Virgin in the church at Vlacherni in Constantinople in the early tenth century, when the city was under threat of Saracen invasion. During an all-night vigil, the holy fool Andrew and his disciple Epiphanios saw the Virgin high above them, surrounded by saints and praying fervently while spreading out her veil over the faithful. Strengthened by this vision, the Greeks overcame the Saracens, and the feast has been kept since then.

Tavener's piece entitled *The Protecting Veil*, written in 1987 for 'cellist Steven Isserlis, celebrates explicitly the Mother of God's cosmic power as manifested by this vision. The solo 'cello represents her unending song, and plays almost continuously throughout the work; the string orchestra, rather than having an independent role, is used really as an extension of this song, providing an harmonic help.

Though Tavener does not consider the work programmatic, the structure is derived from a series of 'sound ikons'. The first represents (rather than describes) her beauty and her power over a shattered world, the second her birth, the third the Annunciation, the fourth the Incarnation of her Son, the fifth (for unaccompanied 'cello) her lamentation at the foot of the Cross, the sixth the Resurrection, the seventh her Dormition (or falling asleep), and the eighth returns us to the beginning, finishing with a musical representation (string glissandi) of the tears of the Mother of God.

Given the ecstatic nature of the work and its non-developmental structure – at odds with the traditional conception of the concerto – its length (nearly an hour) could have militated against its success. It is the more impressive then, that Tavener's work has made such a strong impact on the public and spoken so directly to so many people, of whatever religious or philosophical persuasion.

The Australian composer Peter Sculthorpe has repeatedly pointed out that the western concept of musical 'development' is extremely restricted in both geographical and chronological scope, and plays no part in many of the world's great musical traditions. In the West alone, 'development' does not occur in chant, or in the music of Pérotin, Machaut, Victoria, Satie or Messiaen, for example; in the East it is similarly accorded no role in the musical traditions of India, Turkey, Japan or Bali, to name but four. Sculthorpe's own work naturally eschews such 'argumentative' construction, and so does Tavener's. It has done so, indeed, from his earliest works, and 'block' construction can be said to characterize his output all the way from early pieces such as *The Whale* and *Celtic Requiem* to *The Protecting Veil*.

As well as being 'mystical', prayer is also earthly, incarnate. The prayer of the Mother of God as she witnesses the crucifixion of her Son penetrates to the depths of human suffering. Tavener's music in his *Lament of the Mother of God* is, in essence, a simple melody ascending a further step up the scale each time it is repeated. By repeating our lament we purge our suffering, as the singers of the *miroloy* in Greece know to this day. The music accompanies the transfiguration of this text of deep anguish into something beyond the human plane (and yet deeply rooted within it, for still incarnate) by the anticipation of the joy of the Resurrection. This is fundamental to Holy Week as celebrated in the Orthodox Church. The Alleluias have already begun: never is there any sense of utter despair, never does the dead man hanging on the cross obscure the certainty that He is also the Son of God Who will rise again. The Mother of God asks 'dost Thou change my grief to gladness by Thy Resurrection?', and this soaring, searing line elicits the firm response from the choir: 'Rise, O God, and judge the earth.' The final 'Woe is me, o my child' is a remembrance of the human fragility of the woman who was chosen to be the Mother of God, and whose lament has been transfigured by the certainty of the Resurrection.

Although we are experiencing not liturgical time but extra-liturgical time, Tavener's music, operating as he says in the *temenos*, the sacred space outside the Temple, brings us into the realm of the sacred. In setting these words of anguish sung before the Cross, it also brings the sacred to the earthly realm. There is a sense in which any music (whether chant or more obviously composed) aspiring to the sacred must 'incarnate' its text; hence the ability of Tavener's music to avoid the merely sentimental. He has understood, like Stravinsky, and like at least two other contemporary composers, Arvo Pärt and Henryk Górecki, that musical restraint, a 'stripped' vocabulary, is the most appropriate means of answering this challenge.

God is with us, a short 'Christmas proclamation' written for Winchester Cathedral Choir in 1987, has a text taken from the service of Great Compline, celebrated on Christmas Eve in the Orthodox Church. Its powerful chant-like melodic lines celebrate the Incarnation using words originating in the Old Testament prophecies, something of great importance, as has already been observed, in the liturgical texts of the various Orthodox rites. Though musical instruments are prohibited in the Orthodox Church, the present work is a non-liturgical setting written for an Anglican choir. Tavener accordingly introduces the organ unexpectedly at the end to reinforce the massive sound required from the choir announcing the birth of Christ.

Very much a product of its text, both formally and musically speaking, is *Ikon of Light*, written in 1984 for The Tallis Scholars. The centre of this piece is a setting of the Mystic Prayer to the Holy Spirit by the tenth-century St Simeon the New Theologian, who believed that the indwelling of the Holy Spirit was something attainable by every Christian. Each invocation of the Prayer begins with the Greek word *elthe* – 'come' – addressed directly to the Holy Spirit. St Simeon's vision of light – the light of the Holy Spirit – is translated by Tavener in musical terms by a melody passed from voice to voice and elaborated until the whole choir alights on a richly luminous chord. The string trio which separates the choral sections represents the 'yearning of the soul' towards this transfiguring light. The entire work is very directly oriented towards the numinous, whole movements being dedicated to the words *phos* (light), *dhoxa* (glory), and *epiphania* (shining forth). Musically, in contrast with the central Mystic Prayer, these movements are shining, static chords – pillars of sound with varying degrees of simple melodic elaboration acting, once more, as metaphors for the words they set.

'It is only the Hidden Treasure I mind about in its beggar's clothes, as if it were music, and not a living, wounded life.' It is with these words written by Mother Maria that Tavener prefaces the score of his *The Hidden Treasure* (dating from 1989), and goes on to explain the genesis of the work:

> I dreamed *The Hidden Treasure* in the form of twenty-five notes which I immediately saw as a Byzantine palindrome representing 'Paradise'. These twenty-five notes formed the structure of my piece, which represents a journey from Paradise towards Paradise; the constant memory of the Paradise from which we have fallen leads us to the unknown Paradise which was promised to the repentant thief. The steps of the Passion and Resurrection of Christ are suggested throughout.

So once again we have a musical and spiritual journey, spread over twenty sections (or 'steps') but in a single movement, 'dancing' towards salvation. Are those twenty-five notes the music of Paradise? I should say rather that – again – they were a metaphor for Paradise, in the same way that music can also be a metaphor for an ikon. The arching opening melody contains a sense of yearning for that Paradise lost. A Paradise myth is common to religions from all over the world (as Joseph Campbell's monumental work has shown), but it is rare indeed in the twentieth century to be given with such conviction so immediate a vision of Paradise (a hidden treasure indeed, since we know nothing of how it will be).

Paradise is glimpsed in the *Akathist of Thanksgiving* in a similarly concrete way. An *akathistos* is a long hymn used in the Orthodox rite, prescribed liturgically in the modern Russian use to be sung at Matins on the Saturday in the fifth week of Great Lent. The prototype *akathist* (others were written later) is addressed to the Mother of God and was written during the seventh century. The text Tavener sets is not liturgical, but was written strictly according to liturgical structure by Archpriest Gregory Petrov in a Siberian prison camp shortly before his death in the 1940s. The poetry is remarkable, for the quality and variety of its life-affirming imagery as much as for the fact that it was written at all in circumstances of such adversity.

The centre of the work for Tavener is the 8th *Kontakion*, a hymn of praise in ecstatic cascades of melody ('Across the frozen chain of centuries I sense the warmth of your breath divine') which is interrupted by a solo counter-tenor singing 'I see your Cross, your Cross for my sake. My spirit in dust before the Cross.' Out of this penitential vision of the Crucifixion praise returns, and we glimpse Paradise: 'Now is the triumph of love and salvation, Here praise unto the ages does not cease. Alleluia.'

Unworthiness, unreadiness to enter Paradise – the Heavenly Bridal Chamber, as the imagery of Orthodox Holy Week expresses it – is the recurring thought in *We shall see Him as He is* (1990). The opening 'cello solo (which returns, amplified by other 'cellos during the course of the work) is in fact a Russian chant, that of the *Exaposteilarion* from Matins of Monday to Thursday in Holy Week: 'Your bridal chamber I see adorned, O my Saviour, and I have not the garment that I may enter in; O give light to the raiment of my soul, Giver of Light, and save me.' This is complemented, however, by the constant assertion of the refrain 'We shall see Him as He is', an expectation of the divine vision in Paradise.

As with so many of Tavener's works the structure of *We shall see Him as He is* (subtitled *Ikon of the Beloved*) is related to a series of ikons. In the final one, the eleventh, the voice of St John is heard, fervently imploring the Lord to come (marked by Tavener in the score 'with the deepest, quietest longing') in a gently chromatic ascending melody, answered just as softly – but with certainty – by the choir: 'We shall see Him as He is.' The final word is given to a high solo violin, which recalls the opening 'cello chant, yearning for the Beloved: 'We have no fitting garment to enter the Heavenly Bridal Chamber.'

John Tavener's work, provocative since he first became known in the late 1960s, has raised many questions for many people during the course of the last twenty years or so: questions about the function of music in today's society, about the nature of religious art, about communication. There may not be concrete answers to these questions, but any art capable of provoking thought on these matters, of at the very least hinting at the 'hidden treasure' (something true of other artists whose work Tavener admires, such as W. B. Yeats, Cecil Collins, George Seferis, and David Jones), is rare indeed and should be valued accordingly.

Ivan Moody

Picture Acknowledgements

Page 1   *St John the Baptist*, Cretan School c. 1600

Page 9   *Christ in Glory*, Tver School c. 1500

Page 21   *St Nicholas 'the Wonderworker'*, Pskov School c. 1500

Page 27   *The Saviour*, Northern Russian School c. 1600

Page 35   *The Protecting Veil*, Novgorod School c. 1500

Page 43   *The Old Testament Trinity (The Hospitality of Abraham)*, Moscow School 16th century

Page 51   *Prophet Jonah*, Byzantine 14th century

Page 59   *Archangel Gabriel*, Tver School 16th century

Page 67   *Deposition*, Novgorod School c. 1500

Page 77   *Christ Teaching the Doctors*, Novgorod School 1475

Photos of ikons courtesy of The Temple Gallery

Contents of Compact Disc

Holiness

1. MARY OF EGYPT 'Bless' duet from Act Three (7:20)

   Choristers of Ely Cathedral, Britten-Pears Chamber Choir, Aldeburgh Festival Ensemble, cond. Lionel Friend, Patricia Rozario (soprano) as Mary, Stephen Varcoe (bass-baritone) as Zossima

   Ⓟ Lambourne Productions Ltd 1993, from 'Mary of Egypt', Collins Classics (Coll 70232).

Psalms

2. I WILL LIFT UP MINE EYES (5:49)

   St Paul's Cathedral Choir, cond. John Scott

   Ⓟ Hyperion 1991, from 'Hear My Prayer' (CDA 66439)

The Mind

3. THE LAMB (3:30)

   The Sixteen, dir. Harry Christophers

   Ⓟ Lambourne Productions Ltd 1993, from 'The Sixteen at 16', Collins Classics (Coll 14052)

4. THE REPENTANT THIEF Final Refrain and Third Dance (3:53)

   London Symphony Orchestra, cond. Michael Tilson Thomas, Andrew Marriner (clarinet)

   Ⓟ Lambourne Productions Ltd 1991, from 'The Repentant Thief', Collins Classics (Coll 20052)

Ikons

5. TO A CHILD DANCING IN THE WIND First Movement: 'He Wishes for the Cloths of Heaven' (4:41)

   Artists include Patricia Rozario (Soprano)

   Ⓟ Lambourne Productions Ltd 1994, from 'To A Child Dancing in the Wind', Collins Classics (Coll 14282)

Mother of God

6. THE ANNUNCIATION Extract (3:33)

   Winchester Cathedral Choir, cond. David Hill

   Ⓟ Virgin Classics Ltd 1994, from 'Thunder Entered Her' (VC 5 45035 2)

7. THE PROTECTING VEIL First Movement: 'The Protecting Veil' (8:41)
London Symphony Orchestra, cond. Gennady Rozhdestvensky, Stephen Isserlis (Cello)
(p) Virgin Classics Ltd 1992, from 'The Protecting Veil' (VC 7 59052-2)

Prayer

8. LAMENT OF THE MOTHER OF GOD Extract (6:53)
Winchester Cathedral choir, cond. David Hill, Solveig Kringelborn (Soprano)
(p) Virgin Classics 1994, from 'Thunder Entered Her' (VC 5 45035 2)

Three Prophets

9. GOD IS WITH US – A Christmas Proclamation (5:16)
Choir of St George's Chapel, Windsor Castle
(p) Hyperion Records Ltd 1991, from 'S₂

Light

10. IKON OF LIGHT Sixth and Seventh Movement
The Sixteen, Members of The Duke Quartet, dir.   ...ophers
(p) Lambourne Productions Ltd 1994, from 'Two Hymns to the Mother of God & Ikon of Light',
Collins Classics (Coll 14052)

Holy Week

11. THE HIDDEN TREASURE Extract (5:51)
Chilingarian Quartet
(p) Virgin Classics Ltd 1994, from 'The Last Sleep of the Virgin' (VC 5 45023 2)
12. AKATHIST OF THANKSGIVING 'Kontakion 8' (6:56)
Westminster Abbey Choir & BBC singers, dir. Martin Neary, James Bowman and Timothy Wilson
(Counter tenors)
(p) Sony Classical GmbH 1994, from 'Akathist of Thanksgiving' (SK 64 446)

Gospel Thoughts

13. WE SHALL SEE HIM AS HE IS 'Ikon XI' (4:21)
BBC Welsh Chorus, The Britten Singers, Chester Festival Chorus, BBC Welsh Orchestra, cond.
Richard Hickox, Patricia Rozario (Soprano), John Mark Ainsley (Tenor), Andrew Murgatroyd
(Tenor)
(p) Chandos Records Ltd 1992 from 'We Shall See Him As He Is' (Chan 9128)

Total duration of CD – 75:46

All extracts used by kind permission

John Tavener's music is published by Chester Music Ltd, a division of Music Sales Ltd.